Dean Forest Stories

by

Ralph Anstis

First published in Great Britain in 1992 by
Albion House, Coalway, Coleford, Glos.

By the same author:

The Story of Parkend, a Forest of Dean Village
Warren James and the Dean Forest Riots
The Industrial Teagues and the Forest of Dean
Around the Forest

Artwork and printing by
M. D. Jenkins Printers, 53/54 Lydney Industrial Estate, Glos. Tel. 0594 844666

To
Winnie and Syd

ACKNOWLEDGEMENTS

I should like to thank my wife Bess for her help and suggestions, and John Anstis for the illustration on page 12, drawn especially for this book.
The illustration on page 111 is reproduced by permission of the British Library.

CONTENTS

INTRODUCTION

There is the press of history in the Forest of Dean in Gloucestershire. Once its industries - coal pits, iron mines, stone quarries and furnaces - were carried on vigorously if incongruously among its trees. Now they have gone, but the ghost of their former existence still pervades.

Walking through the Forest I often wonder about the people who, centuries ago perhaps, lived in this house, walked along those paths, worked in that abandoned pit. What were they like? What sort of lives did they lead? The basic facts about some of them can be extracted from record offices and church registers; but even so their essential character can seldom be discovered, and we can turn them into credible people only by using our imagination.

In the first three of these short stories I have taken facts that I have discovered about people who once lived in the Forest and clad them with imagination. The original names of the characters who inspired the stories have been retained, so do not be confused if the same Forest name turns up in more than one story.

The last three stories have more fiction than fact in them, though they, too, are set in the Forest.

LATE FOR THE SHIFT

The background to this story is the flooding of the Union Pit on Thursday 4th September 1902. Four men lost their lives in the disaster, but five others were rescued, three after being entombed underground for five days. The description of the disaster is based on contemporary newspaper reports, though some of the facts have been altered a little to fit the dramatic requirements of the story. Though Joe Price and Tom James both worked at the pit and Tom was killed in the disaster, details of their story are fictitious. The pit was never used again after the flooding. I have been told that after the disaster Dean miners, fearing bad luck, never went back to the coal face for anything left behind.

My thanks to Maurice Bent for reading the text and making suggestions.

PETER TEAGUE

The story of Peter Teague's involvement in timber stealing in the Forest in 1804 is confirmed in official documents in the Public Record Office. His working in Potlid colliery for a year and a day to become a free miner is confirmed by his application to be registered as a free miner in the Gaveller's Office in Coleford. The story traces part of Peter's life as he went from uncertain youth to confident and successful coalmaster, which local history books tell us he became.

As well as the Teagues, all the characters in this story were real people - Moore, Ellway, Tovey, Blunt and John Beech, even Phil the tough one!

THE KITCHEN MAID

This story is set in the first part of the 19th century, and is about Hannah James, sister of Warren James, the man who led the riots in the Forest of Dean in 1831 and whose efforts to bring a better life to his fellow Foresters resulted in his being tried for felony and transported for life to Tasmania.

Anyone who doubts that a poor miner's daughter from the Forest could become the mistress of a member of the aristocracy should know that it is reasonably well established that the real Hannah James was living with an aristocrat in London in 1831 and that her brother insisted that he had met Lord Lowther when he was Chief Commissioner of Woods and Forests and therefore minister in charge of the Forest of Dean. After his capture he refused to say anything about his 'London connections', though information about them might have reduced his sentence. It may be that he refused to give details about them at his trial in order not to implicate his sister.

THE MINERS' FUND

The characters in this story are fictitious, though Uncle Bill is based on a Forest miner who, during the 1926 miners' lockout, was shamefully blacklisted after speaking up at a meeting called by colliery owners. But though the characters are fictitious, memories of the lockout linger in the Forest of Dean to this day.

THE TEA SHOP

This is the story of a Forester who left home when she was in her teens. She comes back after a prosperous life in the outside world to retire in the Forest.

PIRATE TREASURE

I was once told that the famous privateer, Sir Henry Morgan, buried some Spanish treasure in the Forest of Dean. This story is based on that unlikely tale. I am indebted to F. A. Cruikshank for his *Life of Sir Henry Morgan* and to Peter Earle for his *Sack of Panama* for the facts about Morgan and Jamaica that I have incorporated in the story.

I should like to warn anyone inclined to go caving in the Scowles, or indeed anywhere else, that to do so without an experienced caver is dangerous.

Ralph Anstis
Coalway, Forest of Dean, Gloucestershire
September 1992

'The Albion was the most disreputable beerhouse in the village'

LATE FOR THE SHIFT

Sally got up, breathed heavily, and purposefully made her way over to Joe. She looked up at him, her little eyes gleaming.

Joe leaned over the side of the pigsty and patted her. She smiled. People don't know that pigs can smile, he thought.

"So you wants another apple, then, do you?" He reached into his pocket and produced one. Sally took it and crunched contentedly.

Joe smiled. It was a slow, lazy smile, which softened his grey-blue eyes and animated his square, cleanshaven face. His lemon coloured hair, straight as a brush, fell over his forehead as he leaned on the pigsty wall and contemplated his beloved pig.

She was a Gloucestershire Spot. The best breed there was. Joe patted her firmly, and marvelled yet again how tough her back was and how bristly her hairs. He gave her a really hard pat. The pig enjoyed it as much as he did. Strange, he thought, his hands were rough from coalmining, yet they seemed delicate against her hide.

But Sally was getting enormous. Alas, the time was coming when she would have to be killed. Perhaps in two weeks' time. Joe had already asked the village butcher to be ready with his knives, and Tom would help. It would be a hard day's work. But the reward! Blood in a jug for black pudding, brawn made from the head, delicious faggots from the liver and lights, fresh pork for a time, and the rest salted down for the winter, with hams hanging up by the chimney. Then there would be a leg for Tom and his dad, a bit for the butcher for his trouble, and something for the grocer for allowing pig-meal on tick. And of course, the pig's bladder for the village children to play football with.

"Are you coming in for your tea, then?" A voice from the back kitchen broke into his thoughts.

"Oh aye," he said slowly.

"Well, come on or you'll be late."

Emily turned back into the house. He stood contemplating the pig for a few seconds longer, and then followed her.

After the autumn sun outside, the kitchen was dull. The baby was asleep in the cradle by the window. The dog basket was, as usual at this time of day, vacant. Its canes were split and jagged, and the dirty worn cushion in it still bore the shape of its missing occupant. Strange, Joe thought, she never washed the dog's cushion nowadays, though she was forever washing everything else. But she didn't like the dog.

He sat at the table. Plate, knife, spoon and cup and saucer were before him. Alongside was a sugar bowl, a milk jug, butter and a bread board on which was half a coburg loaf. There was no table cloth, but the table was scrubbed so thoroughly that the grain stood out dark against the whiteness of the wood.

Emily was kneeling before the range pouring boiling water slowly into the teapot. She said nothing. Her face was motionless. Then she replaced the tea caddy on the mantelpiece, and took the teapot and a soft boiled egg in an egg cup to the table.

Joe contemplated the egg, and waited for the tea to brew. He sensed her coolness, and searched for something to say. He saw the oil lamp, a present from her granny, on the dresser, its glass shade resplendent with its large painted roses and dark green leaves.

"I see you've bin polishing the lamp," he said pleasantly.

"I do polish it every week," she replied.

She poured his tea. Then she repositioned a hairpin, jabbing it hard into her bun. Joe knew that she did this when she was het up.

"I wish you'd re-paper the kitchen sometime," she said. "I can't abide they violets, and it's all coming away in the corner."

"I will sometime," he said, though he knew that the wallpaper was not the cause of her coldness.

"If you spent more time at home and less at the pub, you could do more things about the house, like," she said.

He was silent. He knew he was responding like a cushion but he was confident he had won the upper hand. For he could see she realised that she had gone too far.

"It's thic Tom James you go with. That's who it is."

"What be wrong with him?"

"He be no true friend of yours."

"Let me decide that."

"I can't say as I like him, with his black hair all greased back. Mrs Marfell next door reckons his grandparents were gypsies. You can see his face is all brown. Other colliers have pale skin through working underground."

"He don't deny it."

"She says he uses butter to spruce up his moustache."

Joe laughed, and looked at her.

"Are you jealous of Tom?"

Emily blushed. "Of course not. But him be a bad influence on you, Joe. You be too honest and simple for the likes of him."

Joe blinked. So she thought him honest and simple. All right, but he was not having her run down his friend. He drank his tea. He was not in the mood for a row today.

His young son, who had come into the room, pulled at his trouser leg.

"Come up, wanna come up." The lad stood, so small and defenceless, at his father's side, a half smile on his lips, his big dark eyes bright with innocence.

"Come on then." He lifted him up, positioned him on one large thigh and put an arm round his waist. The boy sat there thin and upright, and looked questioningly at Joe.

"You want some of Dad's egg, then," he said, and spooned the top of the egg into his mouth.

"I've done your tea and bait," said Emily. "It be bread and butter as usual." Then, making an effort at reconciliation, she added, "but I'll put in a morsel o' cheese as a special treat, like."

Joe reached over and inspected his tommy bag, made from some old curtains and closed at the mouth by white tape. In the bag was a snowl of bread to which Emily added some cheese wrapped separately.

"Good," he said, doing his part to heal the breach. "Cheese toasted over a candle at bait time, a real feast." He placed the bag next to an old whisky bottle filled with cold tea - no milk, no sugar - and checked that the slip knot round the neck was secure.

"Wanna get down." His son wriggled to the ground. Tom tucked into his egg.

"You know, we'll have a bit more food when we've killed poor old Sal," he said.

Her annoyance twisted again inside her. 'Well, that's what we keep the pig for, isn't it? I sometimes think you love that there pig more than you love me."

"Aye, I do love 'er. 'Er be beautiful. But not as beautiful as you," and he caught her playfully round the waist as she turned.

"Not now," she said.

Joe could maintain his good humour no longer.

"It's always 'not now'. It was 'not now' yesterday. It'll be 'not now' tomorrow, I shouldn't wonder. Why can't you be like other men's wives? You won't let me touch you these days."

For reply Emily ran into the back kitchen and shut the door.

What was the matter with her these days? He stared ahead. He was a good husband to her. No-one would deny that. He always handed over his wages every fortnight. Kept a bit back for beer, of course, had to do that. But he didn't drink much. Had only come home really drunk twice in all their married life. And he had never lifted his hand to her, even when he had had too much to drink.

What *was* the matter with her? She had been so sweet when they had been courting. All the young men in the village had wanted her, but he had won her. He remembered when they had walked in the woods in bluebell time. She had worn her best white dress, and her soft honey-coloured hair, smooth and glowing, had surrounded her face like a cloud of corn in the sun. They had lain down among the bluebells, she a whirl of blue and gold and white. And her eyes had shone with love, and they were the only ones in the world.

Then on the way back they had called in at her granny's, and she was the first to hear that they were engaged. He remembered how they had sat in the front parlour on the settee, shyly, hand in hand, as her granny had handed them cups of tea and cake. He had glanced down at her, so neat and small. With her hair drawn back tightly from her forehead, he saw her profile, so delicate, so perfect that he felt an ache inside.

Beautiful too, had been the first year of marriage. They had been lucky to get the cottage, and he had been so proud of her, and the way she managed the house and looked after him, getting his dinner and cleaning his boots, and drying his wet pit clothes every day before the kitchen fire. And then at night when he had bathed and cleaned all the pit blackness from his skin, they would sit close to one another in the glow of the kitchen fire piled high with coal. Or maybe go up to bed early.

Joe cut another slice of bread, placed it on the bare table and spread butter on it. Of course, her looks weren't what they used to be. Her eyes were heavy and her lips were straight and tight. She looked worn, though she was still only 25. But then, things must be different now they were married. She was a good housewife, though. She kept the place neat and clean. He couldn't complain about that. As clean as you can expect with a flea-ridden dog and a collier around the house, she used to say. She didn't make jokes like that any more.

It was after the first baby arrived that things had changed. She no longer seemed to enjoy the love-making and always had excuses. And what was there without that? Well, there was home, of course, but without *that* there wasn't much. You soon get fed up talking about babies. That was all she wanted to do these days, when she talked at all. You got fed up with them crying too. You wanted to get out of the house and go to the pub and see Tom and your other friends.

That was the trouble, it seemed. Emily didn't like Tom. She didn't realise that he was a grand pal. In his company the smallest, most ordinary happening became fun, and the longer they had known each other the more ordinary happenings had bound them together. And when they were at work Tom was good to be with. He was serious then, and a reliable mate. Joe would trust him with his life.

He finished his egg and pushed the plate away. He cut another slice of bread. Well, that was that. Joe wrinkled his nose, and tried to think about something else.

Emily returned. Joe looked up, prepared to be accommodating if her approach was conciliatory, but ready to argue if provoked.

"Joe," she said. She had clearly been crying, and washing her face had not removed the signs. "Joe, it's not that I don't love you."

"What is it then?"

"Joe, I don't want another child, that's what it is. We've got two under two years, and we can't risk a third."

So that was it. Didn't want another baby. It was out at last. He didn't want another baby, either, for that matter. It was a pity that babies came from love-making.

He shrugged his shoulders and ate his slice of bread. The silence was painful, but was soon broken by the baby in the cradle. Emily picked him up and made soothing noises. She stood by the window jogging him in her arms as she looked away from Joe up the village street. She had to say something.

"Tom James have just come round the corner."

"Then I must go," he said, relieved.

He brushed some crumbs off his moleskin trousers, reached for his waistcoat, jacket and cap from behind the door and put them on. He picked up his carbide lamp, and checked that he had six candles for the shift in his jacket pocket. Then he put his muffler round his throat, picked up his tea bottle and tommy bag, bade her a quick goodbye and hurried up the garden path. He ran the last few yards and jumped over the gate. The iron studs on his boots hit the stone paving with a clatter as he bumped into Tom. They both laughed and slapped one another on the shoulder. Tom replaced his cap at its usual perky angle.

"Watch out, old butt," he said, his dark eyes gleaming. The two men went down the street, with their tea bottles and tommy bags over their shoulders.

Down the middle of the village street they marched. No cringing on the side for them. They owned the world.

"Where's Amos, then?" said Joe. Amos was Tom's younger brother. He was one of their trammers.

"Him be gone on ahead, like," said Tom. For a few minutes they marched on in contented silence.

Then Tom said, "It's me birthday today, you know. Look what the old boy give me."

He produced a silver watch from his pocket. Not a new one, it was true, but a beauty. It was large and solid and gleamed from much polishing.

"You be lucky," said Joe, as he took it in his hands and admired it.

"Aye, he's a good fellow, me old man. In spite of all his troubles, he's a good chap."

At the crossroads by the Britannia they saw three colliers approaching, one large, one medium, one small.

"Here be Bill and the two Berts," said Tom. "Why their father ever called one Albert and the other Herbert I can't guess."

The big collier was Bill Martin, a burly man with massive chest and strong muscles, an asset in coal winning. His large liquid eyes in the clean-shaven, pork-pied face peered closely into yours as he addressed you in his loud, insistent voice. He was lecturing his slighter colleagues now.

The bigger of these was Albert Gwatkin, a gentle lad of 18. His ears stuck out in a friendly manner, and you could not quarrel with him. His body was spare but well built. His over-large collier's clothes, probably handed down by his father, made him seem bigger than he was. He had only recently achieved a place on the coal face at the Union Pit in the same stall as Joe and Tom. His brother Herbert was his trammer. He was 12, only out of school a few weeks, and not yet aware of what the world was all about. His face was pale and thin, and his boots seemed too heavy for his legs to manage. When they joined Joe and Tom, he gazed up at his brother as if seeking guidance.

"Hallo young Herbert," said Tom, and put his arm round his shoulders and gave him a squeeze. "How yer feel today, then, all fit for a good night's work?"

"Yes, thank you Mr James."

"We be all mates together now, Herbert. You just call me Tom like the rest on 'em."

Joe did not think Herbert looked at all fit for work. He remembered his own first few weeks in the pit. He had come home so tired that all he wanted to do was climb into bed. Sleep was so warm, so cosy, but the nights were so short and the days so long. Joe had heard that Herbert's mother had feared they had made a mistake in putting him in the pit. But his father had been right in saying that all the boys were like that at first and he would soon get used to it.

The five colliers walked on abreast, filling the road. At the Crown - the village was well served with public houses - they took a path that led to the woods. Outside the Albion, another pub, the last house in the village on the very edge of the woods, Tom stopped.

"As it's me birthday today," he said, "do any of you fancy a drink before we go on? There be time."

Joe thought it was a good idea, but the other three declined.

"Can't work proper, like, full o' beer," said Bill Martin, and they continued down the path into the woods.

The Albion was the most disreputable beerhouse in the village. Hard drinking and coarse manners prevailed. Yet it was friendly and cosy. Tom and Joe went down the side to the tap room entrance. There was a front door, but nobody used it.

Joe looked round the room. All was quiet and orderly, for it was early in the evening. Oil lamps, not yet lit, hung from the beams. The room was still relatively clear of tobacco smoke. The floor had been strewn with sawdust from the nearby saw mills. Joe noticed that over the bar next to the old photograph of Queen Victoria was a new photograph of the new king.

A few old men and disabled miners sat on the benches around the walls, talking and smoking behind their mugs. Two dogs in the corner began to fight over a bone. One of the miners got up and stopped the quarrel with his boot.

Tom spotted his father at his usual table in the corner. "Let's sit with me dad," he said. A small, sunken man was Mr James, his gaunt head seemingly a size too big for his narrow shoulders. A widower, old before his time, worn out by forty years of coal-mining, he waited with resignation for the next blow life would deal him.

He waved. "Come over here, boys," he said, eager for a chat, for time hung heavily with miners too sick to work. But the mere utterance of these few words started him coughing. His eyes closed and he concentrated his whole being on the force that had taken over and was racking his body. His heart pounded. He lost all interest in everyone and everything. He was utterly absorbed with coughing. Eventually deep from his lungs he hawked up a blob of black mucus and spat it into a cast iron spittoon filled with sawdust.

"Dammed coal dust," he said simply, and wiped his eyes and mouth with his handkerchief.

"Aye," said Joe. What more could one say? Most miners succumbed to 'the dust' in the end.

"Be yer going to the union meeting upstairs tonight?" Mr James asked Joe. There'll be some cock fighting arter, so they tells me."

"No," said Joe. "I be like Tom. I be on the night shift."

The barmaid, a comely blonde girl of about 18, came over for the orders. Her plain brown dress was generous in its folds below her slight waist, but it closely enfolded the upper part of her body. Here breasts stood out warm and alive as she placed one hand on her waist. She looked at Joe and then at Tom. She stood, Joe noticed, on one foot, the heel of the other resting on the ground with her ankle protruding from the hem of her dress.

"Hello, me lovely Lil," said Tom. "Two pints, love. And better have one for the little man here, too."

"Cheeky bugger," said Mr James.

As the barmaid left, Tom nudged Joe and grinned at him affectionately. "Lil's a nice 'un eh?"

Joe did not respond.

"Oh come on," continued Tom. "Don't be so shy. I've seen you eyeing her. You be a bit soft on her, I shouldn't wonder." His eyes shone at Joe wickedly.

Joe, uncomfortable, grinned back. "You be mad for the women, Tom." But he admired his friend's clear-cut, uncomplicated approach to life.

"So be you, deep down, like. But you be too serious. You thinks too much, that's your trouble." He clapped Joe on the shoulder.

Lilian arrived with the beer.

"Thank you love," said Tom, patting her neat bottom affectionately. Lilian struck his hand away with a swift and well-practised movement of her arm.

"Stop it, if you don't mind," she snapped. The tone was fierce but the whole operation was routine.

"Leave the girl alone," said Mr James. "Behave theeself."

"That be three pence," said Lil. Tom gave her the money with a wink.

"Nice watch you give Tom for his birthday, Mr James," said Joe.

"Oh aye. It be a good un. Me father give it to me when I were 21, but now I can't go down pit no more, I got no need of it. Keeps good time, too, that it do. Only loses about a minute a day. Yer needs a good watch in the pit."

"How old was you when you first went down, then?" asked Joe.

"I were eight years old when I did start. Pulling hods underground, I remember."

"Get away," Said Tom. "'Twasn't legal."

"Legal or not, I was eight year old, I tell 'ee." He sipped his beer, his rheumy eyes seeing back into the distant past. He sighed and then began to cough again.

"Cough it up, old chap," said Tom affectionately. "That be what comes o' buying you beer."

Mr James continued to cough, concentrating all his energies, indeed his whole being, on the operation.

"Have another drink, Mr James," said Joe in sympathy.

Though still coughing, Mr James managed to indicate his acceptance. Joe went to the counter to order another pint.

"Haven't seen you here lately," said Lilian, glancing sideways at him.

"Haven't been here lately."

"Going up to the Crown, perhaps?"

"Could be."

"Like that, is it?"

Joe looked at her. Lovely eyes; saucy, like. Different when she was not responding to the coarse jokes of the customers and fending them off.

"Could be," he repeated.

"You bin dodging me, like?"

"Who would dodge a girl like you, then?"

She smiled slightly, and moved her head sideways a little as she drew the beer. Her large ear-rings moved against her face. There was no doubt about it, she was a lovely girl.

"I reckon you be a bad influence on me," he said.

She looked at him. "Oho," she said, and her face dimpled. "We only chat. There be no harm in having a chat, be there?"

"No?" Joe was enjoying flirting with her.

"Though we can't ever have much of one 'ere, can we, boy?"

Joe remembered Tom's teasing. "I want more than a chat," he said, surprised at his boldness.

"Oh you do, you you?" Her eyelids fluttered. "You want a cuddle as well, I suppose. Well, well, Joe Price."

Joe looked over to see what Tom was doing. "Let's have that pint," he said.

Lilian finished drawing it and put it on the counter. She wiped the slops she had caused with a rag, and looked straight at him. The brassy barmaid disappeared. She like this raw, honest young collier.

"I finish in five minutes," she said quietly. "I've bin here all day, and I've had enough. Annie takes over then, thank God." She took his hand. "What about seeing me for a few minutes outside, then?"

He squeezed her hand in response.

"Meet me round the back, then, eh?" she said.

Without a word, Joe threw a penny on the counter, and took the beer over to Mr James, whose coughing fit had now subsided.

"Come on," said Tom, getting up. "It's taken you long enough to buy thic pint. We'd better be off."

They left the beer house. Then, with no more than "I'll catch you up," Joe disappeared round the back.

Tom paused and thought for a second. "Don't be late for the shift," was all he said, and walked on. At the edge of the woods he glanced back, but Joe wasn't in sight. He shrugged his shoulders, and with a grin continued on the path through the trees towards the pit.

Joe had only a few minutes to wait before Lilian appeared. Hair combed and all spruced up, she hurried over to him.

"I mustn't stay long, you know," he said.

"Just a few minutes, then," she replied, and led him into some stables by the side of the beer house. The horses were standing in their stalls contentedly munching their oats, and resting after their day's work. Lilian raised the hem of her skirt, and made her way delicately up the ladder to the hay loft. Joe followed, excited.

All was dark and mysterious. She turned to look at him as he reached the top of the ladder, smiled and dropped backwards onto a pile of hay. The moon shone on her face through a small window in the roof. She patted a space beside her.

"Come 'ere and sit for a minute," she said. Her blonde hair lay around her head, soft and delicate in the moonlight. He lay down next to her.

"There be more 'bout you than I thought," she said. Her lips beckoned. Her breasts rose and fell. The smell of hay mingled with the fragrance from her skin as he gazed at her face. "Thinking 'bout it be the same as doing it really, you know," she continued.

The blood came up in him. He had a desire to touch her, an urge for mastery and satisfaction.

"I'll show thee what there be in me," he replied with a grin, and took her in his arms. Her soft flesh yielded to his hard body. Then there was laughing and giggling and a flurry of petticoats.

Later, in a daze of peace and tenderness, he became conscious of the horses moving quietly below and the distant sound of revels in the inn. Then he realised where he was and where he should be. He kissed her quietly on the forehead, collected his things and crept from the hay-loft.

It was now quite dark. As he went back past the pub he could see the oil lamps in the tap room shining yellow through the windows, and he heard a burst of laughter from inside. Glancing through the window he saw some of his friends from the day shift. He smiled. They had stopped off on their way home to clear the coal dust from their throats with beer. Now they were teasing Annie, the barmaid. Indignant, she looked, her black eyes gleaming, her red lips parted in a retort. There was more laughter, and she flounced off behind the bar, with a toss of her head. Joe could see old Mr James, still in his corner, quietly enjoying the scene. He smiled, but he did not envy them.

He walked off in the direction of the pit in an exhilarated mood, swinging his tea bottle and tommy bag as he went. He thought about Lilian and her caresses, and the warmth and relaxation she had induced in him. Then he remembered Emily. No, he did not want to think about Emily, not now. Better think about the excuse he was going to give for being late for work. He would be at the pit head in less than half an hour. Then there would be another twenty minutes walk underground to join his butty Tom at the coal face.

What would he tell Tom? The truth, of course. Tom would laugh and punch him jokingly in the ribs. Tom would understand. He would be a good friend, as usual.

Joe took a path to the left and began the descent into the valley. Behind the black feathery lattice of the trees he could see the honey-coloured moon just past its full mellowness, bouncing up and down as he proceeded with long strides down the path. Soon he would no longer feel the evening cool brushing his cheeks. He would be underground where the tunnels would ring with the noise of trams and the voices of his mates.

But under the earth, he thought, there were also other tunnels that did not ring to the swing of a mattock or reflect the light of the briefest candle. There were miles of such tunnels, worming their way in and out, up and down, crossing and re-crossing, all made over the centuries by his ancestors in their search for coal and a living. But they had yielded up their coal and were now abandoned. Year after year they had stood, dripping with water and slowly caving in, their roof timbers rotting and collapsing. But they were not dead, not silent, for the earth groaned as it moved, and the rotting timbers creaked as they yielded slowly to the pressure of the earth. And all was dark. Darkness, thought Joe, was the most terrifying part of pit life. Whether you had your eyes open or closed, there was absolute blackness, complete, impenetrable and obliterating. Nothing was so black as pit blackness.

Meanwhile at the pit the night shift had already begun. John Harper, the examiner, had started his first tour underground on the lower road. The men, stripped to trousers and boots, were straining and sweating at the coal face. Sighted moles they were, Harper told himself cynically. They would toil to earn sustenance to enable them to toil again the next day - to toil until their strength and manhood had been leeched away by unremitting labour. Then, no longer of use to the pit owners, they would be thrown aside. Young Herbert Gwatkin, arms like yellow sticks, strained past, pushing an empty tram. Undernourished boys like this one became undernourished men before they were 13, he thought. Then they would take over from their fathers, and the pit owners would transmute the coal they hewed into gold.

He pushed his gloomy thoughts aside. In fact, it pleased him to see the men's candles flutter black shadows on a blacker wall and their head-lamps glance, now here now gone, on the shiny grimed bodies of their mates. He was pleased to hear the trams clanging on the rails, the men's mattocks ringing on the coal and their voices, rough and encouraging, echoing from the coal face. These sights and sounds comforted him. In the depth of the hostile earth he was in touch with life.

A draught of cold air struck his face. Concern replaced contemplation. Someone had left a ventilation door open. He must deal with it. The light from his head-lamp zigzagged from wall to wall and from floor to ceiling, and he followed it with a quick eye. As he went up the incline he noticed that a rivulet of water was trickling along by the wall. He put on speed. Twenty yards later he traced its source in the gob at the end of the level. Water was spouting out of a crack. As he inspected, the crack spat out pieces of coal and water began to gush out as if from a tap.

"God," said Harper. "Flood," he bellowed. "Leave your stalls. Get out. Flood." He ran back down the level shouting to every stall.

The men looked up from their work. Bewildered at first they soon comprehended and ran out, shouting to their mates. Urged on by the water now swishing round their boots, they went, in two and threes, down the roadway. Some set off for pit bottom, some disappeared into the black holes of the connecting ways to the upper level.

Those who ran up the connecting ways escaped the flood. Those who hurried along the level found it getting angrier and louder as they went. It was menacing their ankles now. Soon it was gushing down the road like a thunderstorm and in a twinkling it was knee deep. And there was still nearly a mile to go to pit bottom. They began to run.

Albert and Herbert were among the last to leave their stall. Albert pulled his brother along, but Herbert was slow by nature, and they were soon well behind the others. Herbert was bewildered, and he stumbled and hurt his knee. Albert put his arm round him, as he had when he was a child, and encouraged him along. But the water, dark, oily and villainous kept throwing them off balance. The noise of the water was frightening, and soon they could hear nothing but the water, the noise of many waters, and the crash of timber hurtling along on the waves. A tram pounced on them from behind and hit them aside as it sailed remorselessly on. Herbert's lamp went out. The water became deeper every minute. Soon it was up to their chests and they were being carried along by the flood and knocked against the road sides. The unloving water embraced them hard, and strove to draw their heads down to its bosom. But gasping, they managed to keep their heads above water and reached the cage platform. No-one else was there. Albert left Herbert and climbed up over the sump and pulled the knocker to summon the cage. When he turned round Herbert had gone. He moved his head all ways to shine the light, but all he could see was rubbish floating on the water. Rough, choppy and black, it rose higher and higher.

"Herbert! Herbert!" But the noise of the water drowned his voice, as it seemed intent to drown everything and everybody.

"Herbert, where are you?" He thought of plunging down into the blackness to search, but he could not swim and knew that he had to keep his head above water for the light. The water lapped angrily round the platform like a thousand dogs that would not be appeased.

The cage came down. Unwilling to give in but realising that he had no strength left, he collapsed into it.

The last man to reach the roadway was Bill Martin. He felt deserted, and was frightened by the torrent as it swept past. He decided to cross the roadway and make for a cutting which led to higher ground. As he tried to cross the flood he slipped and his lamp went out. Seized by an eddy, he swilled along, the sides of the road snarling and snatching at him. His strong body was of no use to him. He grabbed a pit prop that was supporting the roof and hung on with both hands. The roar of the water was deafening. The flood, cold as an enemy, was now up to his chest, and he could smell the stale slime of the water. He looked round. Ahead the lights of his comrades were scurrying away. Then they disappeared and all was black. No reflections arose from the waters as they thundered by. The current jerked at him and he thought he must let go. His bleeding hands slipped and he slowly fell below the raging froth of the torrent.

Just before Joe reached the valley bottom he took a short cut through the trees. Slithering down the bank, he came upon the back of the pit's engine house. The whole colliery was surrounded by trees, and when he came this way, he was always surprised how quickly he came upon the pit.

All was quiet when he entered the pit area. Around the edge, nestling under oak trees, were the corrugated-iron engine house with its chimney stacks belching smoke, the check-weighbridge, some nondescript buildings, including the carpenter's shop and the office, and the pit shaft with its head frame standing menacingly over it like a guillotine. Scattered around in apparent confusion like the discarded toys of a giant, were rails and trucks, some full of coal, some empty, untidy coils of wire cable, stacks of pit props, heaps of coal and cinders and a miscellany of rusty pieces of mine equipment. Over everything was a thin coating of coal dust.

Jim Baldwin, the engine man, was outside the engine house adjusting an oil lamp. He turned and eyed Joe suspiciously.

"Old Cooper be looking for you," he said. "Why so late, then?"

"Got delayed," said Joe.

"Delayed? Only one thing could delay you and your mate Tom James, I reckon. A bit of skirt on the side, I shouldn't wonder."

Joe was repulsed by the coarseness of the remark. Then he realised that this, in fact, was what his escapade had been. But the realisation did not make the taunt any more acceptable. "Very funny," was all he said.

"Price!" It was Cooper, the pit manager, emerging from the office and moving at speed in spite of his bulk.

"Inside. I want to talk to you." Joe entered the office. As he was taking his brass check disc off its hook he heard an urgent summons on the pit-shaft knocker.

"No coals be due yet," said Jim to Cooper. "Who do want to come up at this time of the shift?" He went inside the engine house. The cage was already at the bottom of the shaft so he only had to set the machinery to bring it up. The big wheel in the head frame began to turn, winding in the rope attached to the top of the cage. The engine panted and strained.

"Must have a full load," commented Jim.

When the cage arrived at the top, men and boys were packed in so tightly that they had difficulty in lifting the iron bar across the cage entrance to get out. Exhausted, dirty and soaking wet, most still wore only their trousers and boots. Faces were smeared with coal dust mixed with blood. Eyes shone white and stared with pain and fatigue. The first man out of the cage, who had been the last man in, was Harper. Joe stared at each man's face as he left the cage. Tom was not among them.

"What the hell is this?" demanded Cooper. Several men began to talk at once.

"One at a time."

"Water's broke through at the end of Point heading," said Harper. The manager took in the implications immediately, and ordered the two pumps at the bottom of the shaft to be started at full speed.

"They'll clear it," he said confidently. "Then after a bit we can go down and see what's what. But where are the rest of the men?"

Before anyone could reply, he was off again. The pumps had stopped. They were clogged with sludge and bits of wood and other rubbish.

The manager cursed. The situation was getting beyond him. He sent someone to fetch the colliery owner, and returned to the men. They were in groups on the ground, some talking quietly, some sitting silently, shivering from damp and dazed with shock.

"I reckon the water bust in from the old workings at Miles' level, you know," said Sam Edmunds, an old collier who had worked underground for 40 years.

"Can't have," said Cooper. "There's 30 yards of coal between them workings and us."

"More like one yard, I reckon," said Harper. 'Somebody must have worked it out all wrong."

Cooper was not inclined to argue, and looked round. "But where are the rest of the men?" he asked again. "Don't tell me they're all still below."

"We didn't leave nobody behind," said Harper. Leastways, I didn't see no-one still coming."

The other men murmured agreement.

"Some must have gone up the connecting ways to the higher road," said Sam.

'Or further on, like, along the windroad,' said Harper, "and then out on top at Futterhill."

"Or happen they be sitting down there on a ledge somewhere, waiting for the water level to go down," said Sam. "If they've found a pocket of good air, I reckon they'd be sensible to stay there till we do get to 'em. But mind you, if they runs into foul air, I don't give much for their chances. I 'spect a lot of black damp have come out of the old workings."

The knocker went again for the cage to be lowered. When it reached the surface again they found Albert Watkin on the floor, semi-conscious. Pieces of wood, rubbish and scum surrounded him.

"Herbert be dead," he whispered.

They carried him to the office, wrapped him in a blanket and plied him with hot tea.

Joe turned away. So Herbert was dead. What of Tom? Footsteps could be heard through the trees. Colliers who had been caught up in the flood but who had escaped along the ventilation adit and other exits now began to come in and tell their stories.

An office clerk made a check of the discs. "Ten men missing," he said and produced a list. As each name was read out a groan arose. "Amos James," continued the clerk. "Thomas James."

"God, not Tom," breathed Joe.

"And Joseph Price."

"Not Price," said Cooper. "He's here."

Harper, who had not noticed Joe's presence, looked at him and his clean face and dry clothes, and said "How did you get out, then?"

"He didn't go down," said Cooper shortly.

Embarrassed, Joe turned away.

"Well, let's not talk," said Cooper. "We need a rescue party." Volunteering hands shot up, many belonging to men who had just escaped from the flood. Cooper selected five reliable and experienced men, including Joe, who was the freshest man present. Harper was put in charge.

"It's no good going down in the cage to pit bottom," said Cooper. "The water will be too high. You'd better start at the adit."

The rescue party fixed their lamps to their heads, and armed themselves with mattocks, shovels, bandages, blankets, and drinking water and brandy for any survivors. Joe took his bait of bread and the cheese that Emily had given him for any survivors, and someone took the milk that the office clerks had brought in for their tea. "Hard luck, butties," they said as they departed.

It was a two-mile walk to the adit. As they trudged through the Forest and over the hillsides, the men were calm outside but agitated within. They felt the press of their collier forefathers whispering their support and telling them that in their time they, too, had searched for their butties. And as the men pressed on they felt the cold, pitiless presence of those treacherous underground forces that could not be reasoned with and could only be vanquished with determination and strength, and not always then.

Joe tried to imagine what he and Tom would have done when the alarm had been raised, if he had been there. They would have been working alongside one another in a confined space, lying full length on their sides, holing out under the coal with their mattocks so that it could fall and be removed by Amos, their trammer. Holing was hard work. Naked to the waist, they would have been, with sweat making rivulets in the coal dust that coated their bodies. Then the alarm would have been given, and they would have crawled out as quickly as they could, leaving their candles in the crevices where they had placed them for general light, but carefully ensuring that their head lamps were firmly in place. And then what? Would they have gone further along the road towards the air shaft? Or up a connecting way to the higher road? Or back to pit bottom like the others who had reached safety? Herbert Gwatkin had done that, but he had not survived. Had Tom James and his brother been behind Herbert and, like him, perished?

The search party reached the ventilation adit. Years earlier it had been the entrance to a prosperous coal level. Now it was used only to provide air for the Union Pit. The over-growing trees and bracken made it difficult for them to find the entrance in the moonlight, but the maintenance men had kept it clear. They paused only to light their lamps. Then they passed in single line through the stone entrance, still neat and symetrical, still strong after a hundred years of weathering. There was moss on the walls and fern growing here and there between the stones for a few feet, and then dampness and gloom took over. The tunnel was too low to walk upright in, and they walked with their heads on one side rather than lean forward, so that they could control the direetion of their head lights. The wet arch of the tunnel reflected the flickering lights into their eyes as they walked along. The occasional remarks they made in subdued voices sounded hollow and amplified.

They were going a little uphill, and on the left was a gully along which rusty-coloured water flowed to the tunnel entrance.

"That's not flood water, any road," decided Joe.

At the fork they went right, along the cutting that had been made to link the old workings with the Union Pit. Wooden supports now replaced the stone archway. The gentle slope upwards levelled off, and in a few yards twisted to the right and began to descend.

Harper stopped and lit a candle from his head light. Holding it low he advanced slowly. "Go easy," he said. "Don't kick with your feet, or you'll stir up blackdamp, if there be any." The candle went out, and they stopped. There was foul air - black damp, the killer that suffocated.

"Turn carefully," said Harper, "and go back."

Defeated, they trudged back towards the entrance. At the junction with the old workings Harper glanced down the old roadway. A few yards along the slope, a white face stared at him. He ran towards it. "Tis John Evans," he shouted. A few feet behind was Arthur Teague. Both men were on their stomachs, crawling up the slope, exhausted. They carried them to the tunnel entrance, where fresh air revived them. They were given some brandy and water and wrapped in blankets.

"Thought you wouldn't see us," whispered Evans. "We were too weak to holler."

"How did you get into the old men's workings, then?" asked Harper.

"God knows," said Teague. "When the flood started we left for pit bottom, but the water knocked us over and put our lights out."

"We managed to get ourselves into an old stall," said Evans. "Didn't know where we was. We felt our way on our hands and knees, just crawling in the dark. For hours, it seemed. We 'ad no lights and didn't know where we was. Just crawling in the dark. Could have landed up anywhere."

The party returned with the rescued men to the pit head. Their arrival there after three hours' absence was greeted with a cheer from the small crowd of relations that had now gathered. Joe's eyes searched for Emily. He had a sudden urge to hold her. But she was not there. He could, however, see old Mr James standing a little apart from the crowd, his hands clasped in front of him, silently waiting.

Joe went up to him. "We be going down again as soon as we can," he said. "We'll get them out." But confident though he hoped his voice sounded, his heart was not so reassured.

Mr James looked at his face, but said nothing. Joe put his arm around his shoulders. Though full of emotion, he could give no greater sign of sympathy.

The pit owner, Thomas Deakin, had been told of the disaster and had now arrived at the pit. Deakin and Cooper were considering the next step. Something was being done about the pumps, but it was clear that no-one could get to the pit bottom until the waters cleared.

"But we can get into the upper roadway," said Joe. "That shouldn't have water in it. And then we can go down the side roads connecting with the lower level."

"Don't be daft," replied Cooper. We can't get to the upper roadway. It goes from the bottom of the pit. It goes up, just as the lower road goes down."

"Yes," said Joe. "It do now. But before the alterations was made it went off from the shaft about 30 feet above the new pit bottom. The entrance was closed up, but we can break through, like."

Deakin confirmed what Joe had said, and agreed that an attempt should be made. A second rescue team was selected. It was led by Cooper and included Joe, who insisted that he was still the freshest man there.

Armed with sledgehammers to break down the closed entrance, and food and drink for any survivors they might find, they got into the cage.

Joe felt the click of the cage being released, and then it dropped 250 feet like a stone. He had gone down in the cage hundreds of times before and was used to the sickening feeling in his stomach and the air being torn from his lungs, but never before had Jim let them drop so fast. Jim stopped the cage about 30 feet from the bottom. Through the slats under their feet the men could see the water swirling angrily.

"Good thing we haven't got to go much further," said one.

"But we have," said Cooper. "Drop another few feet," he bellowed to the top, and the cage dropped to where the closed-up entrance to the upper level was.

They broke through, and were soon scrambling into the disused roadway. They searched it as they advanced, listening for every sound, but they met no-one along the whole of its length. Disappointed, they stopped at the top of the last passage connecting the two roads.

"If we go down here we should be near where the waters broke in," said Cooper. "The ground's higher there than at pit bottom, so the water won't be so deep."

They descended the slope cautiously. Soon they could hear the water lapping. They stopped at the edge and listened.

"Sounds as if all the water that be coming have come," said Joe. They descended further and turned into the lower roadway. The water came up to their ankles, but no higher. It was calm now, with just a few ripples lapping up against the sides of the road. But it looked hostile, with debris of tommy bags, knee pads, bits of wood, a miner's shirt, all floating limply on the surface, exhausted by the buffeting they had undergone. A dead rat floated by, its hard, cruel eyes open and staring. A few feet away a dead cat followed, no longer in chase, but resigned and uncaring. Enemies once, they were now indifferent in the anonymity of death.

Smashed trams littered the floor, broken pit props, no longer performing the function they had been put up to do, leaned askew. Staccato drips from the roof into the muddy waters played an obligato to the swish of the men's legs as they walked slowly forward.

They went down the Slade heading. Joe looked into the stall in which Tom would have been working and in which he should have been when the flood started. There was no dust now. Everything was covered with a moist, sticky black paste. There was no-one there, only the water lapping against the coal face. A few mining tools lay on a shelf of natural stone where they had been placed at the beginning of the shift.

Joe went on. The others followed. They moved their heads from side to side, searching for any sign of a human being, and as they searched they feared that they might find one. As the road went downhill the water became deeper. It now reached the calves of their legs, and they realised that they must search the road bottom for bodies as they went. They walked abreast so that every inch was covered. Every time they encountered a lump they reached down with their hands to discover what it was. On and on they went, slowly in their loathsome task.

The roadway widened. The water was now up to their knees. After a brief consultation they agreed that the search must be called off until the pumps could reduce the water level. And then, as they were about to turn back Joe raised his head and the light from his lamp shone further down the level. He could see a faint shape high up on the gob. On hurrying nearer he saw that it was two bodies, two men lying in the mud, drowned. Their legs were in the water, and they were holding each other as if to comfort themselves in the awful moment of death. Joe's stomach tightened with a feeling of sickness. It was Tom and Amos. His eyes filled with tears. He forgot it was unmanly to cry.

When the alarm had been given, Joe decided, Tom had sought out his brother, and they had fought the flood together. Tom's laughing black eyes were closed now. His rosy face was pale and a frown sat on his forehead. With trembling hands Joe picked up his cold, inert body in his arms. The strong firm muscles that had wrenched so much coal from the earth were slack, the body, sodden with water, was heavy. It slipped through Joe's grasp and fell with a splash into an awkward heap at his feet. Then with a start, Joe realised that both

Tom and Amos were fully clothed. They had gone to where they had left their clothes -their vests, shirts and coats - and put them on before fleeing from the flood. And they were only 15 feet from a passageway to the upper road.

As Joe lifted Tom again, his light picked out the reflection of something in Tom's left hand. It was his newly-acquired watch. So he had stopped to go back for that, too. Joe prised the watch from the clenched fist, and put it in his pocket for old Mr James. If they had not gone back for their clothes and the watch they might have been saved. If he had been there, he would have stopped them, he knew he would. Oh why had he not been there!

The walk back with the bodies was a mile of recrimination against himself and anger against a world that allowed such murder. Why did men have to go into the cold wet filth and darkness of a pit to earn a living, and a poor one at that? His anger focussed on the colliery owners. They had caused the rape of this Forest, covered it in coal dust, fouled its pure air with smoke, polluted its sparkling streams with fish-killing mine water, deafened its quiet with the noise of engines, and heaped on its green hillsides the ugly sterile slag, the obscene, unwanted entrails that had been wrenched from the earth. And now incompetent officials, he was sure, had failed to ensure the safety of those who gained the coal and had caused men to die. But then, Joe concluded, men were cheap to replace.

As the party reached the cage, he pushed these thoughts from him. He remembered Emily. He had betrayed her just as he had betrayed Tom. And both with the same deed. Emily! He wanted to hold her close, and the two children. Things had been difficult recently, he knew, and it hadn't been all his fault. But he could have made more of an effort to understand.

He recalled his escapade with Lilian. Had she tempted him or had he gone up the hay-loft steps willingly? Whichever it was, the adventure had brought no lasting satisfaction. And he knew that if he had not gone up those steps, he would not have this feeling of guilt, this ache in his being. But he *had* done it, and that was that.

Perhaps it was not so very important. The men would certainly dismiss his lapse with a laugh if they found out, though he would not tell them. They always laughed when they heard of such events, good-naturedly on the the surface, but really in an uncomfortable way. They were not sure, but they had to pretend they ruled the roost and could do no wrong. And they had to show contempt for the women involved.

But, he thought desperately, Emily need not be hurt. She need not know. His secret, raw now, would heal with time, leaving only the knowledge that it had shown him where his love lay.

When the cage jerked to a halt at the top, Joe was the first out. The bodies of the dead men were taken to the office. A crowd of several hundred people had now gathered. A barrier had been erected to keep them away from the pit head.

They murmured fearfully as they pressed forward, anxious to know the names of the men brought up, and whether they were alive or dead.

Joe narrowed his eyes and looked for Emily. He could see only old Mr James patiently standing where he had been earlier, his hands clasped before him. Joe walked over to him.

"I'm sorry," he said. He handed him the watch.

Mr James took it, and looked up with sad, unblinking eyes. Joe realised he need say no more. Mr James quietly and slowly made his way to the office.

It was now four o'clock. The moon had gone down and there was only the splash of light from the solitary oil lamp hanging outside the office to focus on. A cool breeze enveloped them. Joe shivered. The search had been long, the concentration severe. The searchers were worn out.

"Go home and get some rest," said Cooper. "We must wait for the pumps now."

Joe was turning to go when Emily ran up, her coat flapping in the dark, her eyes wide and strained.

"I came down as soon as I could find someone to sit with the kids," she said. "Oh, my Joe. You're all right, aren't you?" She searched his face as if she was not certain it was him.

"Yes, I be all right." Oh, to feel her warm softness in his arms after so much hardness, cold and wet! To feel her straining against him so lovingly after their encounter the previous evening in the kitchen.

He closed his eyes for a minute. Then, "Let's go home," he said.

They walked slowly, arm in arm, up the side of the valley to the top. They said little. The dawn rose behind them, chill but clean, giving promise of a beautiful autumn day. Birds chorused their welcome to the sun.

"Oh, Joe." She clutched his arm. "I don't know what I would have done if you had been killed." She paused. "They say there be little chance for the others still below."

Joe was silent.

"If they haven't been drowned," she continued, "the foul air will have got them. That's what they say."

"True," said Joe.

"It be awful about Tom and Amos." She paused. "Tom wasn't such a bad chap really."

"No," said Joe.

"And poor Mr James. All alone now."

"Yes," said Joe.

They reached the Albion, deserted and exhausted after its customary night of revelry. Emily stopped, and faced Joe.

"Joe," she said. "Weren't you with Tom and Amos when the flood came?"

Joe paused. "I didn't go down with them. I was late for the shift."

"Why was that, Joe? You left home in good time."

"I was - er - delayed. Else I would have been with them."

Emily shuddered. "That would have been awful. But you weren't. Oh, Joe, I'm so glad. Never mind what delayed you, I'm so glad."

Under the oak trees outside the Albion she hugged him close. He put his arm round her and pressed her to him as they walked home.

PETER TEAGUE

The atmosphere changed the moment James came into the room. Moses and Isaiah, sitting at a table in the corner, stopped laughing and whispering and, putting on serious faces, got on with their homework. Sarah re-settled herself in her armchair near the fire, took another piece of mending from the box at her side and concentrated on her needle. Peter, who had been chatting with Sarah, leaned back in his chair towards the candles on the side table, picked up his book and began to read. Even the flames of the candles on the tables realised that their flickering must be subdued.

James Teague's sitting room was large and dismal. Its furniture, like its owner, was simple, solid and rustic. The floor-to-ceiling curtains on this particular evening had been pulled across the windows early to shut out the dark cold of the street. But there was no cosiness within.

The carpet, which covered most of the floor, was the only concession to comfort. It had once responded, in a whirl of blue and green, to the quick feet of young people; but now it was old and dull. The floor boards around its edge, however, proud that they were of Forest oak, gleamed, polish-bright, as they waited for better days.

The only outstanding feature of the room was the wrought-iron fireplace. Cast at Coalbrookdale by old Abraham Darby 70 years before, its iron-bridge motif was still a wonder of design to anyone who cared to examine it. Its basket was now brimming with burning coals whose red-warm fingers reached out into the room and overwhelmed the pale flickerings of the candles.

James's face reddened from the fire as he entered the room. He was a burly man, six foot in height, tall for a Forester in the first decade of the 19th century, and thick with it. But he was not fat; every pound was solid muscle. His dark hair was thick and, in spite of his 55 years, barely tinged with grey. His jaw was edged with a short beard that emphasised the squareness of his face. His dark penetrating eyes swept suspiciously round the room, noting who was present and what each was doing.

Sarah glanced up at him coolly and then, smiling in a friendly if guarded way, greeted him. James did not reply, but sat in the windsor chair opposite her at the other side of the fireplace. No sooner had he sat down than he was up again, reaching for the poker. He sent a shower of sparks up the chimney.

"This be good coal, Sarah," he said, and looked at his wife. She was wearing one of her best dresses again, he noticed. This time it was a yellow one. She must have bought it in Cheltenham when she visited her aunt last summer. It had a high waist, practically no waist at all, when you came to think of it, since it started just under the armpits. But he approved. He might be a Baptist, but he could still admire his beautiful young wife, even if she did spend a lot of his money on clothes.

"Did you deal with Mr Tovey, James?" She pronounced the name 'Tuvvy'. Under her brown curly hair her round face came to life as she spoke.

"Oh, aye. He be gorn." He looked round.

"Just sit and enjoy the rest of the evening, James," she said. "It's a pity you can't read very easily. We've got plenty of books, and there's the newspaper."

"I baint interested in what goes on in the papers. I gets on all right without readin'. As long as I can sign me name on cheques and such I be satisfied."

Peter, his son, looked up from his book. He noted with disdain James's dark, no-nonsense jacket with its large pockets, his britches and gaiters and boots, still muddy from the roads, and his long dark-green waistcoat stained with dropped food. He's never been able to read, he thought, so he doesn't know what he's missing.

Feeling Peter's eyes on him, James looked over. "Peter, him do enough reading for both of us," he said. He examined Peter more thoroughly. He was 17 now, but not as big as he had been at that age. He looked grown-up this evening, though, quite self-assured as he sat, affectedly James thought, with one elbow on the arm of his chair and one leg crossed elegantly over the other. He was wearing some new clothes. The coat was chestnut brown and, beneath it, was a striped green and white waistcoat, its brass buttons gleaming in the firelight. A white silk cravat flowed round his neck, and his close-fitting cream trousers had perpendicular slits at the bottom. So this was what he spent his allowance on. All the latest fashion, no doubt, thought James, but he disliked it.

And he did not approve of his hair, either. It glowed fair and healthy, but it was short and dishevelled. Sarah had told him that this was the way the young men in Gloucester wore their hair. But he didn't understand why Peter combed it carefully before the mirror, and then ruffled it. Well, that was the way youngsters did it these days, he supposed.

Peter could see that James was appraising him and, uncrossing his legs, he continued to pretend to read.

James looked away, into the fire, and forgot the new clothes and modern hair style. His problem was how to introduce what he had decided to say to Peter that evening. He wanted to persuade the lad, and not insist, because this was something important. He had done it all wrong with Enoch, and Enoch had gone off as a farm labourer to the other side of the Forest. Every time he thought of Enoch he recalled his obstinacy and that day especially. He recalled his bull neck and his rough face, red with emotion, and his eyes blazing as he had shouted back at him. Enoch was like himself.

But Peter was different. James would get his way with him, of course. There was no doubt about that. Peter took after his mother, James's first wife. She had been easily persuaded. He looked a bit like her, too. She had been fair and had had delicate features. But she had never been a really fit woman, God rest her soul.

"Peter, I wants to talk about what you be goin' to do, like, now you've left school."

"Yes, papa."

"I let you go to school because your step mother here wanted it for you and the other boys. I couldn't see much in it meself, like. Learning all that Latin and Greek, didn't seem much use to me, but I could afford it and I wanted you brought up right. But now you've left. You be a man now."

Peter looked at him squarely.

"You 'ave known all along that you would be coming into the business like the other boys eventually."

"Yes, papa." There were a dozen other jobs he would have preferred, but he knew that to mention them would have no effect.

"To take over from me, you 'ave to learn the trade, you know. I got where I be not only by 'ard work, but by knowin' what I was doin', and what the others was doin'. I did start at the bottom, lying in the mud and dirt in the pit diggin' out coal wi' me 'ands. At your age I 'ad been in the pit for nigh on ten years."

He held out his big hands with their thick spatulate fingers. They no longer grasped coal, but the scars stood out white on the rough brown skin.

"I wants you to learn everything about the coal trade from the bottom up," he continued. "You can learn the office work later, but first I wants you to learn about being a collier."

"Yes, papa."

"It means getting dirty and roughing it, like."

"Yes, papa."

"I wants you to start at Potlid. You know, doan't you, that when you 'ave worked in a pit for a year and a day you'll be a free miner. Leastways, when you be 21."

"Why a year and a day? Why not just a year?" Peter snatched at the unimportant to delay the inevitable.

"I doan't know thaat. It's always bin a year and a day. Anyroad, when you be a free miner, you can start up pits in the Forest anywhere you fancy."

"Yes, papa." Peter could not conceive that he would ever want to start a coal pit anywhere.

"So you begins in the mornin' then. You'll need some pit clothes. See Ned. He'll fix you up."

"Yes papa."

"I'll be comin' with you, mind, and tell Moore what it be all about."

They rode to the pit the next morning, James on his cob and Peter on the pony that had taken him to school at Newland every day for the last six years. The pit was about five miles away, set on top of a plateau amid trees - oak, beech and sycamore - and bordered by an enclosure jealously fenced off by the Office of Woods to protect their saplings. As James would proudly have told you, it was a big pit, one of the few in the Forest that could afford an engine to raise the coal. James employed twenty men there alone.

They took a short cut through the Forest waste, James first and Peter following. Thomas Moore, the pit foreman, was talking to some colliers by the engine shed when they arrived. He was a well-built man of forty, not tall but tough. He had to be tough to become a pit foreman for James Teague. When he saw James he hurried over. James introduced Peter to him and explained what he wanted him to do, where he was to work and what he expected him to learn. Then, after discussing briefly one or two colliery matters, he was on his horse and away.

Peter watched him go. For once he wished his father had stayed a little longer.

"Come on, Peter, let's go in the office, then." Moore spoke in a hearty way that did not reflect his feelings. But this was the master's son.

He took Peter into a wooden shed. An old kitchen table in the middle was covered with pieces of paper made grubby by coal-grimed hands. At one end were half a dozen partly used candles. In a corner by the side of some pit lamps lay a coat, cast down in a moment of haste and left there. An open fire was burning sulkily in the grate, and light peered uncertainly through a small unglazed window at the back. Over everything lay a coating of coal dust.

They sat down, and Moore lit a pipe. As he puffed to get it going, the interior of the hut became even more loathsome and claustrophobic to Peter than when he had entered.

"So your feyther wants you to be a collier, then."

"Yes, Mr Moore. He wants me to learn the job - from the bottom up, he says."

"Well, that do mean the pit bottom up, doan't it?" He laughed at his joke. "We'll do that, aye, we'll learn you to be a collier. And we'll learn you to manage things up 'ere on the bank, too."

Moore did not have any sympathy for the youth. He had to watch his step, of course, but he would soon have those smooth hands rough and that blond hair dirtied.

"Well, I'd best find someone to look after yer," he said.

He went to the office door and looked across the yard.

"Hey, you, Beech," he shouted, "come 'ere."

A young collier came over. He was about 18 years of age, slim, but taller than Peter and sturdier. His face was thin and black with coal dust, but you could see his complexion was pale underneath. He was clean shaven, his cheekbones and the bridge of his nose stood out, and his hair was nondescript fair.

He stood easily in front of Moore, his eyes relaxed.

"This be Mr Teague's son who 'ave come here to learn to be a collier, like," said Moore. "Now, you 'aven't got no permanent trammer at the moment, so you can 'ave 'im. Teach 'im tramming and then take 'im on the coal face with you and show 'im 'ow to do it."

The young man's eyes laid hold of Peter, and examined him. There was no sign of greeting.

"Find 'im some tools in the shed round the back," Moore continued.

"Yes, Mr Moore," said Beech. When he spoke his white teeth and red lips stood out against his coal-blackened face and softened it. He turned to go. Peter followed him.

Among a pile of pit tools on the floor of the shed Beech sorted out two shovels and passed them to Peter.

"And you'd better have this mattock while it be here," he said. "It be a good one, but you won't need it yet if you be going to do tramming." His voice was deep, his words measured.

Peter took the tools from the man who was to be his instructor. He did not sense in him the animosity of Moore, but there was no indicaiton of friendship, either.

"You bain't be going down pit dressed like that, be you?"

Peter looked at him, almost afraid, and ashamed at the criticism. Beech was probably only a year or so older that he was, but he was bigger and more confident. Peter felt that he was a man, while he was still a boy. "I've got my pit clothes here." He indicated a bundle under his arm.

"Well, best put them on.'

Peter followed Beech across the yard. At the pit head they climbed into a large wicker basket. It was used for conveying coal to the surface as well as taking the men to and from the pit bottom, and the interstices of the wickerwork, broken here and there, were caked with grime. Beech gave a signal to the engine man, the engine spluttered and juddered, and they began to disappear down the square, stone-clad well. The basket swayed from side to side as it dropped.

"Don't put yer fingers over the edge or you'll get 'em crushed," warned Beech. They had not gone far when water oozing from between the cracks in the stone walls of the shaft began to shower on them like rain. By the time they reached the bottom, some 150 yards down, they were soaked. Peter realised that he would remain wet and uncomfortable until he reached home that evening, and looked at Beech for comment. But Beech did not seem to have noticed the downpour.

Peter wished he knew what to call him. 'Mr Beech' was wrong, and 'Beech' seemed condescending. How did labouring people address one another?

Beech had clearly been considering the same problem. "Do you want me to call you Mr Teague or by your Christian name, then?" he asked.

"Oh, Peter, please."

"You 'ad better call me John, anyroad." He smiled just a little, as if pleased that that difficulty had been overcome.

Peter soon learnt how to do tramming. It consisted of shovelling the coal hewn at the coal face into a tram and pushing it to the pit bottom. But though it was easy to learn, it was hard to do. It made Peter's muscles agonisingly taut, and he went home every night exhausted.

After a few weeks John Beech took him off tramming. A permanent trammer had arrived, a 14 year old boy called Harvey, with bulging muscles and a grin that, even though it revealed broken, discoloured teeth, was always cheery. After seeing how John worked the new trammer he suspected he had dealt leniently with him. Perhaps he had been sorry for him. Peter did not want that. He thought he had made little of the hardships that he had not been brought up to expect.

Peter now began to learn the technicalities of the pillar and stall method of coal getting. In his slow, solid way John was a good teacher, explaining the work gently and patiently.

"Now you try," he would say.

But Peter was clumsy. Once when John was guiding his hands with his own, Peter realised how warm, big, rough and powerful were the other's, and how smooth, unblemished and small his own were under them.

"They tells me you've been to thic school at Newland," said John. "But they didn't teach you much about getting coal, did they?"

Peter laughed. Warmth flowed between the two youths. It was John's first joke, and Peter was pleased to have a joke made against himself. After that, relations were easier and Peter, using intelligence to make up for lack of dexterity, proved a satisfactory learner.

He soon realised the importance of co-operating with the other colliers in his gallery. Some were willing to be friendly, but others were suspicious. Him being the boss's son, anything they said might get back to James Teague. But Peter was passionately on their side. He knew the dangers they endured, the hardship they encountered every day and how little was their reward. He wanted them to know this, but could not tell them.

This was a new world of relations to him. At bait time he appreciated the warmth and humour, broad though it was, and the feeling of comradeship that often enveloped them as they sat, Peter included, on one heel with the other leg stretched forward, munching their bread.

Though Peter was glad to be taken off tramming, he found work at the coal face almost as tiring. But the exercise developed his muscles, as he discovered when he examined his body when alone in his room at night. Then he realised that using his muscles when he worked gave him satisfaction; and he decided, as he watched John, that he too got a similar satisfaction. Unconsciously, as he walked along the underground roads and at the top of the pit, Peter adopted the slouch the other colliers had. He felt he was now a man, proud of his manhood.

During those weeks Peter and John got to know each other better. John was never subservient and treated him as an equal, but he was careful never to be too familiar. His manner was unpolished, though he had a natural politeness that gave him dignity.

Peter, for his part, wanted to pleased John, but was wary of showing it. He felt humble in the presence of a skilled craftsman, for that was what he considered John to be. He did not appreciate that John would flounder in his own world of books and sophisticated conversation.

One day John called him 'thee'. Peter thought that this meant that he was accepted as an equal. But was it a mistake? Had he really meant it? Peter regretted that he could not reciprocate, but he had never addressed anyone in this way, and it would be hypocritical to attempt to do so now. John never 'thee'd' him again.

Nevertheless, he wanted to become more friendly with John. He wanted to invite him home, perhaps to tea one Sunday, but he knew that his father, heavy like a bear, would not approve. Peter sensed that John would also like to be friendlier, but he was not sure. He seemed so complete, so content with life as it was.

So caution separated the two, an awareness not to go too far. But gradually the barrier lessened. It never disappeared. At bait time, when on occasion they would sit apart from the other colliers, they would tell each other about small things they experienced outside the pit. Peter was cautious not to emphasise his more comfortable background, but he would talk about his young step-mother and his brothers, Moses and Isaiah, those two awful old testament prophets, as he called them. He seldom mentioned his father.

John told Peter about his family, how his father had been killed in the pit some years back. His mother had taken on the job of collecting the charges at the toll house at Berry Hill to keep the home together. John, her only child, was about ten at the time of the accident. He was working at Potlid, and had been since he was five.

Peter thought it was a great privilege when John confided that he was courting a girl from his village. She was called Effie, was 17 and tended the cows in Mr Dobbs's dairy. Peter asked what she looked like.

"Well, she be small like, and fair," was all John could offer. "We hope to get married one day, but not for some time, I shouldn't reckon." Peter dared to say that he would like to meet her. John looked surprised. "Yes, one day you must," he said. Peter hoped that was a promise.

Peter wondered if John had ever tumbled Effie in the bracken, though he did not, of course, dare ask. He hoped he had, but he did not know why.

Peter knew several girls from the well-to-do Trotter, Thomas and Birt families in Coleford, and since he had left school, he had been allowed to go to the monthly dances at the hall in the Market Place. But though one of the Trotter girls had dropped her handkerchief once for him to pick up, he was not attracted to her or to any of the others. Peter wanted to know so much about girls. Perhaps he would ask John sometime; he was sure to know.

Then, just as their relationship was beginning to develop, Moore told Peter that he must come above ground and learn the organising and accounting side of pit work. Sitting in the dirty office with Moore and another clerk was easier than slogging at the coal face, but the work was less satisfactory. Peter found little mental satisfaction from entering details of the coal each group of colliers had sent to the surface and working out their money. On occasion he was careless, and Moore grinned when an irate collier queried his pay.

Peter now saw little of John during the day, but he usually waited for him at the end of the shift, and they would go part of the way home together. It was summer now; and tired and relaxed they would slowly walk in the early evening sun - a benison to colliers condemned to darkness all day - hearing the birds preparing for their rest, and letting the cool, clean Forest air caress their faces. As they walked along the side of the pike road to Berry Hill, with Peter leading his horse, John would relate gossip from the coal face, and Peter would rail against Moore's ineptness; but they would also talk about everything and nothing, as friends do. When they reached a lane near John's house, Peter would canter down the hill and in five minutes he was home.

One morning there was a knock on the office door. A thin, sharp-faced, wiry man entered. It was John Ellway, one of James's waggoners. Peter knew him. Though not over-intelligent, he was bright enough to do as he was told and make it seem that he was pleased to do it.

"What about thic beech tree in the enclosure, then, Mr Moore, sir?" he said. "You did say it should be moved soon, like."

"Yes, take it down to the master's pit at Coalway. Mind, though, tha's got to be careful no-one sees thee."

"What tree's that?" asked Peter.

"Oh, it be a tree in the enclosure over there on t'other side of the pit." He indicated vaguely. "It 'ave been lying there for a week. I think we should 'ave it."

"But if it's in the enclosure, it isn't ours, is it?" said Peter.

"What you mean, t'isn't ourn? Your feyther be entitled to Forest timber for his pits free, and always 'ave done."

"Isn't it stealing, though? Blunt and the Office of Woods would have something to say if we took it."

"To 'ell wi' the Office of Woods. And Blunt wants to watch out, with 'is pokin' and pryin' into what goes on round 'ere."

Ellway looked from one to the other uneasily. "Perhaps we ought to leave it, leastways for the present," he said.

"What after all the trouble we took in cuttin' it down?"

"You cut it down?" said Peter, unbelieving.

"You be a green one, green as thic bloody tree." Moore was not used to people disagreeing with him, and Peter had ruffled him. He turned to Ellway. "We'll get some o' they outside to help load it on the waggon and then tha can take it to Coalway, see?"

"What do I say if I meets any o' Blunt's men?"

"What do he say, Peter?" asked Moore sarcastically.

"I don't know."

"Well, you be the master hereabouts," he teased maliciously. "Leastways, you be the master's son. It be up to you." A grin crept over his lips. His earlier discomfort had gone now that an opportunity to embarrass Peter has arisen.

Peter was silent. Moore turned to Ellway. "Do like I tells thee. If tha does meet anyone, not to mention the master's name. Him be in enough trouble with Blunt and the rest of 'em already."

Ellway turned to go.

"I'll come with thee," said Moore. "Cheer up. The master will look after thee if anything 'appens, won't he, Peter?"

Peter was uncertain. "I suppose so," he responded.

Moore and Ellway crossed the yard. Peter watched them from the office doorway, his hand on the door jamb. Moore summoned several men who were working on the heaps of coal to follow him. One was Philip Jones - Phil the tough one, as he was called. Six foot six tall, 20 stone in weight and packed with muscle. He was too great an asset to use on the coal face. His enormous strength was best used on the bank doing the heavier work there. Phil was proud of his abilities, and enjoyed exercising his strength. Yet he was a mild man, careful not to harm anyone by mistake, and with a chuckle like an organ rumbling and a laugh like thunder.

Moore and his men disappeared into the woods. Peter decided to follow. About 100 yards in he found Moore and company climbing over the enclosure wall and approaching the felled tree. A fine beech tree, it was, lying helpless on its side with its branches, their leaves still green and vibrant, sticking out strongly from the trunk and protesting their aliveness. Peter hid behind a clump of bracken. Moore and his men manhandled the tree over the enclosure wall, and began to trim off its branches. Everyone worked with a will, Moore included. Then they were ready to load it onto Ellway's waggon.

They all looked to Phil.

"Come on Phil," they said. "This be your part."

Phil smiled in anticipation of a satisfactory experience. The men raised one end of the dismembered tree from the ground sufficiently high for him to squat under it. He slowly raised his shoulders until they made contact with the tree, and then he pressed up. His face was concentrated on his effort, his eyes were closed. Big veins on his neck stood out. His body trembled, and he began to exude sweat. Streams of it poured down his face. The tree began to rise. The others guided it as Phil staggered towards the waggon. With a quick movement he edged it onto the waggon and the job was done.

Sad at heart, and filled with foreboding, Peter watched until Ellway climbed into his seat, whipped up the horses and drove away. As he turned to return to the office he heard Moore telling the men to remove the branches that had been lopped off.

"We don't want no evidence left behind, do us, lads?" He laughed, and the others joined in dutifully. Only Phil, the tough one, laughed as if he enjoyed the joke.

The evening of the following day Peter arrived home to discover his father's solicitor, Mr Tovey, outside the house climbing down from his horse with much puffing and grunting. He was a middle-aged, spherical-shaped man with short legs, and it was a long way down from the saddle. He pulled his wide-brimmed hat down over his wig, and brushed his coat down. He had ridden over from Newnham, a distance of 9 miles.

"Hallo, young Peter," he puffed. "I've come to see your father. Something important." Peter rang the front door bell for him, and took his horse and his own to the stables at the back of the house. A few minutes later he joined him, his father and Sarah in the family sitting room.

Mr Tovey had recovered his breath, and was fumbling in his pockets. From their case he extracted a pair of oval, gold-rimmed spectacles, put them on and adjusted them carefully. Then he looked over them and addressed James, who was waiting impatiently to learn what the visit was about.

"Mr Teague, sir," he said. His voice was deep, dramatic and resonant. "Mr Teague, you have a waggoner called Ellway employed at your Potlid colliery, I believe?"

James nodded.

"Well, the man was arrested last night for stealing a tree from the vicinity of the colliery."

"That's the tree - " began Peter.

"Peter, let him finish," said his father.

Mr Tovey looked quickly over his spectacles at Peter and then at James. "He was brought before a magistrate this morning. It was Mr Maynard Colchester. Hard luck on Ellway, I must say, because Maynard Colchester believes in dealing with timber stealers severely. Two Office of Woods men gave evidence," he continued. "One of them had discovered that the tree had been

43

felled some days before and had marked it. Ellway was sentenced to 6 months in Gloucester gaol. And that's where the poor, timid wretch is now."

"Did he say who did cut down the tree and ordered him to take it?" asked James.

By now Mr Tovey had somehow ousted James from his place in front of the fire. He had become the centrepiece of the drama, and was adopting the stance that he employed when appearing in court, one hand gracefully concealed behind his coat tails, the other waving elegantly in the air. Everyone was waiting for his words.

"My information is that he said he did not know who cut the tree down, and that you, sir," addressing James, "knew nothing about it."

"But I know about that tree," interrupted Peter, "and so did Moore. Moore ordered him to take it to Coalway."

"God bless my soul," said James. "Did you agree to that?"

"Moore said, 'That's all right, Peter, isn't it?' and I suppose I agreed." He looked at his father, and expected an outburst of anger.

But James was thinking. "Well, let it go," he said. "And do you, Tovey, keep an eye on what is happening and let me know."

"But we can't let Ellway take - we can't leave Ellway in gaol and do nothing," said Peter. "Moore and I promised we would look after him if anything happened."

"Leave it, Peter," said James. He looked at his son disapprovingly. "Leave it. We'll look after him - when he do come out. Not to worry."

Three days later, when the family had just finished dinner, Tovey arrived again, tired, cold and wet. The ride across the Forest in the rain had put him in a bad mood. The two boys, Moses and Isaiah, were despatched to their rooms, and Mr Tovey was revived with a glass of wine. Normally James would have offered him cider, but he judged that wine was justified on this occasion.

A servant took Tovey's overcoat to the kitchen for drying, and the gentleman himself sat by the fire, flapping his trouser legs to dry them.

"Well," said James when he thought Tovey had had enough time to settle down. "What now?"

"Ah, Mr Teague, sir, more trouble, I fear. The wretched man Ellway has confessed all. At Gloucester gaol he told the magistrates that he was ordered to take the tree to Coalway by Moore and - I hate to say it - by young Peter here. Further, my sources tell me, there is now the possibility - nay the probability - of summonses being issued against them." He looked over his spectacles at James as he stretched his feet nearer to the fire and interlaced his fingers over his paunch.

"But Peter didn't do anything, really," said Sarah. "He didn't touch the tree."

"Accessory before the fact, ma'am. Accessory before the fact. That's what they will allege."

Peter turned away, his heart pounding. What did this mean? Prison? How long for? He couldn't deny such a charge. Indeed he wouldn't. It was true. True in a way. But in another way it wasn't. Tovey ought to know all the ins and outs of the law and must get him out of this trouble.

"And," Mr Tovey was continuing, 'to compound the difficulties with which we are confronted, the authorities, so I am reliably informed, have decided that all the evidence was not available at Ellway's trial, and they have released him on condition that he gives evidence against Moore and Peter."

After more discussion, Tovey left. While James was seeing him to the door, Moses and Isaiah came into the room, grinning maliciously. They had been listening at the keyhole.

"Peter's going to gaol. Peter's going to gaol," chanted Moses.

"You'll be eaten by rats and then you'll be sorry you've been so horrible to us," squeaked Isaiah.

"I'm not horrible to you. Go away," shouted Peter.

Sarah shooed them from the room, and went over to Peter. She stood behind his chair and smoothed his hair.

"Not to worry, Peter. Leave it all to your father. He'll see you through." Her voice was gentle.

Peter took her other hand, which was on his shoulder, and pressed it. It was soft and warm. He smelt her sweetness and twisted his head round.

"Oh, Sarah," he said.

She withdrew her hand. "You'd better not let your father hear you call me Sarah," she said quietly. "I may be only seven years older than you, but I am still your step-mother."

Peter shrank back. He needed no reminding of their relationship. But he needed the understanding of a young person together with the tenderness of a mother to console him.

James returned. "Blunt be behind this, for sure," he said. "He 'ave been an enemy of mine ever since he came here in charge of the Forest, and that were 25 years ago."

"I can't see how Blunt could have been connected with it," said Sarah.

"He wants to get at me, and he be doing it through Peter."

"But the tree *was* stolen," said Peter.

"And you could 'ave been more careful, couldn't you?"

'I think *you* could be a bit more sympathetic, James," said Sarah.

"Sympathy be blowed," snapped James. "He'll suffer for this, now. He'll 'ave to suffer. We all 'ave to suffer in life."

He stared at Peter in his anger, and Peter did not recognise that it was the situation that annoyed him, not his part in it.

"But we'll do what we can," continued James. "I've told Tovey to get the best attorney that be going. It'll cost money, but that can't be 'elped."

In a few days Peter and Moore were formally charged before Mr Maynard Colchester, Moore of a felony, Peter for being an accessory before the fact, as Tovey had said. The proceedings lasted only a few minutes, and both were freed on bail pending their appearance at the next Assizes. Tovey paid the bail money, which had been supplied by James.

The summons to attend the Assizes at Gloucester came at last. The day fixed for the hearing was 13 March, a Tuesday. It was a cold morning and barely light when Peter set off. The clouds were low and menacing, and a thin mist swirled round him as he rode through the Market Place and up the Gloucester road, his horse's hooves echoing against the sleepy buildings. He was to meet Mr Tovey at his office at Newnham, and together they were to travel to Gloucester in Tovey's carriage.

Both horse and rider began to glow as they climbed up the hill that led to the Speech House in the middle of the Forest. The building looked more lonely than ever as it stood wreathed in mist, and moisture was dripping off the holly trees that surrounded it. The stretch past the Speech House was a wild part of the Forest, and Peter kept a lookout for robbers. He did not expect any at this time of the day, but had a purse with a few coins in it to hand over if necessary, most of his money being concealed in the neck of his riding coat.

At Littledean the mist began to clear, and people were coming out of their houses to start the day's work. A ten-minute canter down the hill and he was in Newnham. Mr Tovey's house and office were in Passage Lane, near the river. As he knocked on the door Peter could see that it was slow and grey and on the turn.

Tovey's clerk, who had entered the office only a few minutes before, yawned and offered Peter a cup of coffee, only too pleased of an excuse to have one himself. While Peter was drinking it, Mr Tovey came in. He inspected Peter. Yes, he was wearing a new riding habit, and was neat enough, considering he had had to come from the other side of the Forest on horse. Mr Tovey placed great importance on a spruce appearance when appearing before the courts at Gloucester, though he was sure that they had little appreciation of the travelling difficulties and the effect they had on one's appearance in getting there.

He himself had put on his new brown waistcoat. It went from his cravat over his paunch to his thighs. The 22 buttons descended like plums on a Christmas pudding. The line of descent was interrupted only by the glorious curve of his watch chain going from one pocket to the other. He had, of course, put on his best wig. He had refused to abandon the wig in spite of the recent revolution in men's clothing - he abhorred revolutions of all kinds - for he was a respectable professional man, and a wig was the surest sign of respectability these days.

Tovey seized his walking stick, a thick crooked one, full of knobs, and stumped outside. Then it was into his gig and off. The mare trotted clip-clop on the cobbles of the town, and then along the road by the bank of the River Severn to Gloucester. By now the mist had cleared and the sun was shining frostily over the river. The water shimmered and glinted like the scales of a fish in the sun.

Mr Tovey tucked the rug more firmly round his legs and advised Peter to do the same.

"Now, young Peter," he said, "I must explain what will happen today."

'Yes, please, Mr Tovey."

"Before you go on trial you will have to appear before a Grand Jury." The very way he pronounced the words showed that they began with capital letters. "A Grand Jury is made up of magistrates. No judge. They come from all over the county, and their job will be to examine the evidence against you and see if it will stand up before a court. They call it making a True Bill."

"Will you be there, Mr Tovey?"

"No, unfortunately. Only the accused, witnesses and prosecuting counsel can attend a Grand Jury hearing. Now what we must do is make clear to them that you didn't really agree to the tree being taken away."

"But I did."

Mr Tovey waved his hand as if removing the very possibility of Peter's statement.

"Say Moore did all the deciding."

"Shall I be on oath?"

"Yes, of course."

"So I must tell the truth."

"Yes, but -" Tovey made a moue and raising his hand in the air, rotated it a little on the axis of his middle finger.

While Peter was working out the significance of the gesture, they arrived in Gloucester. They drove through the West Gate and in a few minutes were entering the yard of the King's Arms. Tovey would dearly have liked a pint of porter, but a glance at his watch showed there was no time. He bustled Peter across the road, through dingy alleyways and mean streets, to the old court house.

It was a large gothic structure, which had seen the woes of many litigants and the pleasures of few. In the corridor outside the court rooms groups of lawyers, solicitors and defendants stood discussing their cases in low tones and with serious faces. Peter and Tovey sat on a stone bench under a latticed window. There was a stale smell of parchment mingled with one of damp mould. Two young articled clerks, the tips of their high collars digging into their cheeks, bustled by with bundles of papers importantly tied with red tape under their arms. They hurried along, their heads forward, with no time for a glance at anyone.

Tovey took a box from his waistcoat pocket and took a pinch of snuff. He offered the box to Peter, who declined.

'In a few minutes they were entering the yard of the King's Arms'

"Where's Moore?" Peter asked.

"He came yesterday. My chief clerk attended him."

"How did he get on?"

"True Bill." Tovey brushed a grain of snuff from his waistcoat.

'Shall we be tried together?'

"Yes, if they find a True Bill for you. But that hasn't happened yet."

"Mr Tovey," said Peter. "I am most grateful for all you are doing for me."

"Your father's wishes, dear boy."

"I suppose so."

"Yes, your father gives me a great deal of work." He sighed contentedly.

After an hour's wait, a clerk ushered Peter and Tovey into an ante-room. Two uniformed guards stood silently by the wall, gazing ahead. The clerk conducted the formalities of Peter's surrender of bail. Then Peter and Tovey sat and waited. Peter looked at the guards, who continued to gaze at the wainscotting in front of them.

Eventually Peter was summoned next door to the Grand Jury's private room. It was sparsely furnished, but well lit from a large window at the end. On one side, seated on a low platform were about 20 men, the magistrates who formed the Grand Jury. Among them Peter could see Mr Maynard Colchester.

When he entered they stopped talking and looked at him. Peter stood diffidently on a platform before a rail.

In the centre of the room was a large table. It had a baize top, originally green, now grey with ink stains. Heaped in no discernible order on it were files, reports, injunctions and affidavits. Around it sat officials. One rose at Peter's entry, pulled his gown over his shoulder, settled his wig and, looking disapprovingly at Peter, administered the oath to him.

The chairman of the Grand Jury called order, and concentrated his attention on Peter. His dark eyes, sunk deep in his pale cheeks, were liquid and penetrating.

"Peter Teague," he began, "you are here to answer questions from us so that we can decide from what you say, taking into account other evidence we have heard, whether the indictment made against you is valid. That indictment is that you acted as an accessory before the fact in the case of timber stolen from one of His Majesty's enclosures in the Forest of Dean, namely the Buckholt enclosure. The judge of the Assize Court, who will preside at the trial has clarified to us the legal aspects, and has instructed us to make a decision whether your indictment is valid."

He then began to question Peter.

"We understand that at the time of the alleged offence you were working at the Potlid Colliery."

"Yes, sir," replied Peter nervously.

"What exactly did your work consist of?"

"Doing office work, sir."

"How long had you been doing that?"

"About a week, sir."

"Now I understand that the colliery is owned by your father. Yet you were working in the office?"

"Yes, sir."

"How was that?"

Peter was gaining confidence. "My father wanted me to learn all aspects of colliery work. Before going into the office, I worked for several months at the coal face."

The chairman's eyebrows rose. "Did you, indeed."

"Yes, sir."

"Did you conduct the interview with the waggoner, Ellway?"

"I was present, sir, but I did not conduct it. John Moore conducted it. He was in charge."

"Yet in a sense you were above Moore. As the pit owner's son, you could tell him what to do, surely?"

"I suppose so, sir."

"Did you tell him what to do?"

"No, sir."

"Did you agree that the tree should be removed?"

"Not really, sir."

"Did you say that your father would look after Ellway if he were caught with the tree?"

"Yes."

There was a pause. Then the chairman invited other members of the Grand Jury to ask questions. The first was Maynard Colchester. He rose, brushed up his sideboards and puffed out his coarse red cheeks.

"Some people consider that free miners can take His Majesty's timber for their pits as a right."

Peter was cautious. "I know nothing of that, sir."

"Does your father believe he has a right to take such timber?"

"I don't know, sir. My father is a free miner, and knows his rights."

"Are you a dutiful son to your father?"

"I hope so, sir."

"And do what he tells you?"

"Yes, sir."

"Did your father know about that tree?"

Peter felt a sudden shaft of truth hit him.

"I - er - don't know, sir."

Other members of the Grand Jury then asked questions, but nothing more of importance came to light, and Peter was dismissed. He returned to the ante-room, and sat and looked at the warders again.

After a further hour of tension and boredom, Tovey bustled in.

"Peter, my boy," he beamed, "you are free. The Grand Jury decided that there was insufficient evidence to justify a trial. In other words, they did not find a True Bill."

Peter suppressed the cry that was mounting in his throat; but nevertheless tears sprang to his eyes. The tension and anxiety that had been with him for so many weeks was diminished by the utterance of a gasp.

Half an hour later, they were sitting down to dinner at the King's Arms. Mr Tovey beamed at Peter over a steaming plate of steak and kidney pudding. He had his pint of porter by the side; and he scarcely knew which would give him the greater pleasure to start on.

Opposite, Peter also had a pint of porter. Mr Tovey had insisted on nothing less. He had a small portion of pigeon pie before him, but had no appetite. Relief at the outcome of his day's endurances sustained him.

"I gather," said Mr Tovey - he had decided to drink his porter first - "I gather that Moore tried to show that you really gave the order to move the tree as you were the master's son."

Peter listened.

"Ellway came again before the Grand Jury after you, and gave more evidence. He said the order was Moore's, and that you didn't help to load the tree onto his waggon, but Moore did."

"How did you learn all this?" asked Peter. "I thought the hearings of the Grand Jury were private."

Mr Tovey tapped the side of his nose with a forefinger. "I have my sources, young man," he said. "Ellway said one or two disquieting things, Peter, which your father will not be pleased to hear. He said your father knew all about the tree. He had instructed that it should be cut down, and had told Moore to move it to Coalway at some suitable time."

Peter recalled the twinge of suspicion that he had experienced during the Grand Jury hearing.

"Blunt apparently also gave evidence yesterday," continued Mr Tovey. "He said quite openly that he suspected that your father was behind the whole business. I shouldn't be surprised if they take your father to court. But I don't know," he added modestly. "I can't tell." And summoning the waiter, he ordered another pint of porter and a suet pudding.

Peter pushed the plate with his half-eaten pigeon pie away, and refused anything more to eat or drink.

"You probably don't know," continued Tovey, "that while you were still at school your father was taken to court for a similar case of timber stealing. He was bailed, but the Office of Woods in London decided to drop the prosecution as the evidence was rather weak. The report from London said that however desirable it might be to convict him, if he were tried and acquitted, he would be more daring than ever in his timber stealing, and encourage all the others."

"They said that?" Peter gaped, but he was more impressed by Tovey's intelligence service than by what he said. Tovey, reading his mind and finding admiration there, smiled.

"I make it my business to know these things," he murmured.

On the way back to Newnham Peter was silent. Tovey had told him a lot. Was he conveying a message as well? In the light of what Tovey had said, Peter thought over his interrogation. He tried to discover the reasons behind the questions he had been asked, so simple but perhaps so significant. He tried to interpret his answers to the Grand Jury as he thought they would interpret them. Then he felt stunned by the whirlpool of nuances and implications that went round and round in his mind.

Mr Tovey, meanwhile, aided by the steak and kidney pudding and the porter, had slowly declined into delicious sleep. Fortunately the horse knew its way home. They reached Newnham without mishap and stopped outside Mr Tovey's residence. Peter was in no mood for further conversation, and with a few words of thanks set off on his horse for home.

The wind was fresh and it was beginning to rain. It was almost dark, as well, but Peter knew the way back to Coleford. It was the same road that he had travelled that morning.

Was it only 12 hours since he had begun his journey? He had set out a frightened gullible youth; he was returning with unexperienced forces welling up inside him. For anger, kindled in the dining room of the King's Arms, had been growing remorselessly until it was now ready to burst. As he passed the Speech House the rain began to sleet down, and he slowed his horse while he buttoned up the collar of his coat. As he galloped down the hill on the other side, the rain beat hard on his face, smarting it, but urging him on even faster. The physical activity dissipated some of his anger.

The rain eased a little as he reached the bottom of the hill and began to slog up the next one. With the change in speed came a change in thought. What was the purpose of getting angry with his father? With one word, one flash of his eyes, he would subdue him.

He became uncertain, and at the top of the hill he decided he did not want to go home. He was not afraid of what he might say to his father or of his father's response. Rather he was not ready, he had not sorted out his ideas. He decided to see John. He needed John's advice, John's comfort. So he turned right and cut across to the Berry Hill road.

At Berry Hill he found the pike house, even though it was dark and rain was still pelting down. He tied his horse to the fence, and knocked on the door. It was opened by a middle-aged woman wearing a shawl, who screwed up her eyes as she peered into the dark.

"Mrs Beech?" said Peter.

"Yes," she admitted, cautiously.

The wind whistled and the rain blew on her. She moved a step back into the house.

"Who is it Mam?" a male voice said, and a face appeared over her shoulder.

"Peter!" said John. "Come in."

Peter entered and was introduced to John's mother.

"Take yer things off then," said John.

Mrs Beech draped Peter's soaking coat before the fire and, muttering excuses, retired into the back kitchen.

The living room was small, sparsely furnished with a chair, a few stools and a table scrubbed white. On the table was a solitary candle. There were curtains at the window. The floor was paved with large stones from the local quarry, and there was a homemade rug before the fireplace. It was poor, but cosy.

John invited Peter to sit on one side of the table and himself sat on the other. He was in his shirt sleeves, and he rested his arms easily on the table. He was pleased to see Peter.

"And how did you get on, then?" he asked.

"They let me go."

"Tell me, but you looks as if you could do with something to eat and drink first." He stuck the poker in the heart of the fire, and went into the kitchen and spoke to his mother. She came in with some bread and cheese, and John returned with two mugs of ale.

Peter began on the bread and cheese without invitation. Seeing the food had set his innards gnawing, and he realised how hungry he was. John was pleased to give, and was pleased that Peter settled in with no ceremony on this, his first visit to his home.

When the poker was red-hot, John plunged it into Peter's ale. It hissed and the beer bubbled and steamed. Peter drank gratefully.

"Tell me, then," said John. Peter told him of his appearance before the Grand Jury, and then moved on to Tovey's revelations in the King's Arms. John listened, watching the emotions that flitted on Peter's face. He said nothing.

"He misled me. He never told me he knew about that tree." The desire to confront his father that had already surged up again and again that evening surfaced once more.

"I've a mind to go home and tell him I know," he said. "There'll be a row, I'm sure." He paused, uncertain. "But John, do you think that's wise? Should I just say nothing?"

John looked at him curiously for a few seconds. The lad wanted advice, wiser advice than perhaps he could give. Peter was so vulnerable, always had been. Yet in him John could now see a determination that he had not discerned before. He seemed more mature than when he had last seen him. The face was broader, the jaw squarer, the skin coarser, the hair a shade darker and thicker. True he was at the end of a tiring day, but the lines under his eyes were lines of maturity.

"I think you ought to tell 'im what you know, but don't go shouting and raving. If he throws you out, where would you go? You wouldn't have a home, you wouldn't have nothing. What would you do for a living?"

Peter listened. The advice he had wanted from John was now being given. He must listen carefully.

"I suppose you could get a job as a collier in some other coalmaster's pit. One who don't get on with your father would be only too pleased to give you a job - and I reckon there be plenty o' they. But you could do better than that, I should think, with your education. But do you want to go off on your own like that?"

Peter listened, but his mind jumped ahead. "The funny thing is that I don't want to leave pit work," he said. "I hated it at first, because my father made me do it. I was frightened, and I hated him for it. But I came to like it. Not the labouring so much, but the organising." He paused.

"I reckon that I could run a pit well all on my own already," he continued with all the confidence of his years. "I could run a whole series of pits, see they were properly maintained, get the coal to market and sell it. I've had a taste of it and I like it. You know," he was in full flood now, "You know, I used to lie awake at nights, despising Moore with his blustering and bullying, and working out better ways of doing things. And recently I've often listened to my father discussing business problems with his brothers and others - he never discusses them with me - and I've had my ideas on what to do. My father's intention when he dies is - or perhaps I'd better say was - was to leave me a large part of what he owns - and he has lots of pits and a share in an ironworks, as you know. So one day, a large part of his empire should be mine to run as I wish."

"Mebbe you could run them, but you still wants a bit more practice, I should reckon." The humour in John's comment eased its severity. But Peter was not listening.

"When I get my own pit to run as I like, you must come and share the work with me. You must."

John was embarrassed, but smiled. The enthusiasm and generosity that splashed against him hurt.

"Nay, Peter," he said. "I be a collier. The work be hard, but I'm not ambitious for anything else. It's what I was born to. I know what I be capable of."

Peter sobered, drew himself back to real life. He wondered whether John had said that with regret, whether he had anguish for what might have been, or anguish that he had discovered in himself no desire to improve himself. He thought not. John was satisfied with his lot, and was solid and calm as a result.

"You be grown up now," John continued. 'If your father be going to have you 'longside him in his business, he 'ave to treat you as an equal. Now praps is the time to tell him so. I 'aven't 'ad much to do with your father, but he don't mind coming down the pit and talking to the men and getting himself dirty, like. And the men respect him for that."

This was an aspect of his father that was new to Peter. He blushed because John had said it.

"He be a bit of a slave driver, but all the coalmasters be the same, I reckon. But he can't be all bad." He paused. "You know, you can't have everything you wants in this life. There be always something to spoil things. There be always something."

John had spoken. Peter had listened. He felt calmer now. He rose, put on his coat, still steaming from the fire, and set off home.

It was still raining as he reached the house. He handed over his horse to a stable-boy, and entered by the back door. His stride seemed longer and firmer than ever before as he clattered along the stone-paved corridor, through the kitchen and up into the sitting room. Sarah, sitting by the fire, looked up in surprise as he threw open the door and stood there. His coat was open, and its large collar and high lapels framed his head. His face was set firmly and his chin was low. He moved slowly into the room, and threw his hat onto a chair.

His father, on the far side of the room, looked round.

"So they released you," he said.

"Yes, they released me."

"Good. Tovey said they probably would."

"You're pleased, then."

"Of course I be pleased. I don't want a son of mine in prison."

"Not even if he was shielding you?"

Anger spread over James's face. He came up and thrust his face close to Peter's and regarded him menacingly.

"Now see 'ere. I didn't shield behind you." James's lips and nostrils were working nervously.

Peter was afraid, but the emotion that was pent up inside him drove him on. He had to continue.

"Why didn't you tell me you knew all about that tree? You ordered it to be cut down and told Moore to have it moved."

"I didn't lie to you. I didn't deny that I was involved."

Peter lashed out again. "You didn't tell me. That's what angers me. You kept me in the dark, and let me go through all this to save your own skin."

James was silent. He chewed his lip as he thought. He decided to be calm, and sat down.

"Peter, it weren't like that." He looked cunningly at Peter, watching his face for signs of weakness, seeking an opening for a counter-attack. "Peter, I've been in a lot of trouble lately," he said. "Trouble with Blunt and they others in the Office of Woods. I don't deny that I 'ave done some timber stealing in my time. But I reckon I've a perfect right to take Forest timber. I be a free miner and we free miners 'ave always 'ad that right."

Sarah sat silently. She would not intervene. They must fight it out between them. She had never suspected that Peter could be so brave as to tackle James in this way, so fool-hardy. But James was experienced in tough dealing and was a determined man. He had not risen in the world without the ability to fight and fight hard when necessary, not being too careful with the weapons he used. This was the old story of the young challenging the authority of the old, she thought, and the old do not yield easily. If Peter stayed in his father's business after this, she could foresee many such battles.

Peter was shouting. "You sent me down the pit to learn coalmining, but the time I spent there toughened me up in a way you didn't bargain for. And I learnt there that people could be decent and kind. And I learnt it from your workmen." His face became flushed as he strode around the room flashing hostile looks at James.

James lost his patience. He rose and stood in Peter's way. The two looked into each other's face with torment and rage.

They stood in conflict for a time. Then James yielded, and went towards the window and sat in a chair. He had remembered Enoch. There had been a similar conflict with him. God! Not again. All the pain that had resulted from that encounter, all the pain that he had suppressed, re-awoke in him. Peter had always been so submissive. He had never thought he would turn out in this way. He could conquer him, though, if he persisted.

But he could not lose a second son.

Peter saw that he had his father on the hip, and with the hardness of youth showed no pity. He looked down at him sitting silently in his chair. He saw the grey hairs on his neck and the wrinkles on his face. He seemed shrunken. Then Peter had a tinge of fear. Was he glad he had won? Had he expected to win? Had he really wanted to humiliate his father? What would he do with his victory?

James got up abruptly and left the room. Sarah drew the wrong conclusion. But her words were true.

"You've won, Peter. You've stood up to him. He'll respect you now."

THE KITCHEN MAID

So it was back to the Forest. She thought she had escaped from it. Indeed, she had got away for a time, but it had claimed her back.

And here she was, travelling on the same old road that she had come along ten years earlier. Hannah untied the ribbons of her bonnet, leaned back, and closed her eyes. The stage coach lurched into a pot-hole and she opened them again.

They had left the Bell Inn in Gloucester about three-quarters of an hour earlier. On the roof of the coach the four young men who had emerged from the inn at the last minute and climbed up on top were shouting to one another with excitement. Well-to-do, well-dressed youths, they were. Their hair, just the right length for the latest provincial fashion, curled from under their tall hats, and their cravats fluttered in the breeze. They were on a day's outing and ready to enjoy themselves. Periodically they tapped the coachman on his shoulder with their canes and offered advice on how to drive his vehicle. Hannah smiled as she listened.

Inside, the only person apart from herself and her charge was a fat, middle-aged man who was sitting in the corner opposite her. With prosperity oozing from him, he sat leaning on his ebony walking stick with his legs wide apart to accommodate his large blue-waistcoated stomach. The stitches on his trousers strained to keep his fat thighs covered. His tall grey hat was on the seat beside him.

The fat gentleman eyed Hannah from time to time. She could feel his eyes evaluating her. Yes, good class, expensive clothes even though a little on the sombre side for such a handsome young woman. He could imagine her, eyes bright and smiling demurely, entertaining the men. But now her face, a little plump, perhaps, for her slender figure, was tired.

Hannah ignored him and glanced out of the window. "Look," she said, pulling the curtains aside. "Look, Charlotte." The child climbed from her seat and unselfconsciously adjusted the white flounced drawers that reached her shoes. Cautiously, for the carriage was swaying from side to side, she went over to her mother. She was about eight years old and on the plump side. Rather a plain child, thought the fat gentleman, but clearly her daughter. Her dress of duck-egg blue was set off like a jewel by the mother's plain dark skirt. Hannah smoothed down the unruly fringe that covered her forehead.

"Look, you can see May Hill over there," said Hannah.

"May Hill?" the child asked. "It it a person?"

"No," her mother laughed, "it's the name of a hill. When you have passed May Hill, you are almost in the Forest. We shall arrive in Coleford in about two hours."

"Have you been to the Forest of Dean before, child?" asked the fat gentleman.

"No, sir," replied the girl uncertainly, and sat down again close to her mother.

"It is a lovely place," said the gentleman. He moved his gaze slowly to the mother. Hannah lowered her eyes and looked out of the window again.

Her thoughts turned from the fat gentleman to other more attractive men she had known. As her mind flitted over them, she realised that she was evaluating them as possible husbands. She smiled inwardly at her cold approach. She had just had a most frightening shock, and here she was thinking about a husband. Hitherto, she had been inclined to the belief that marriage should be about love. At least that was what her books had told her. But she knew what love had done for her. No, she decided, love was all right in marriage if it came as a bonus. But marriage itself came first. Yes, when she had recovered she must consider marriage. She was only 27, after all, and living alone for evermore with a child and without a man was a frightening prospect. Charlotte needed a father's hand, something she had never had. She must consider marriage and choose carefully. Yes, *she* would choose this time. She had a considerable fortune now, and proposals would no doubt be made. The man she accepted would have to be reasonably young, of course, and not too intelligent. William had been too intelligent - she realised that now - and too well educated. She wanted someone like Charley Kear.

She fingered a simple gold necklace round her throat, and mused for a minute about Charley. The years that had passed softened her remembrance of him. She recalled his toothy smile and cheery presence, and then his coarseness and gawkishness. But Charley had probably married by now, some little maid from Bream, most likely.

No, she decided, Charley would not do, even if he were still unmarried. She wanted someone more presentable, more intelligent, more educated, someone with whom she could exchange views, discuss the newspapers, talk about the latest novels. She was, after all, an educated woman now. She had changed or, to put it more accurately, had been changed since she left the Forest. She could not revert to being a simple Forest girl.

Charlotte interrupted her thoughts.

"Will Uncle Enoch be waiting for us at Coleford?" she asked.

"Yes, Uncle Enoch will be there. I wrote yesterday by express and told grandma that we should be arriving on this coach."

"Do you think I shall like Uncle Enoch?"

"Oh, yes," said her mother, "I think so. He's jolly, and has a little boy and girl of his own. You'll be able to play with them."

"Are we staying with grandma?"

"Yes, for a short time. Then we shall have a house of our own. Just you and me."

"Does Uncle Warren live in grandma's house?"

"No." Hannah paused. "No, not any longer. He's gone away."

"I didn't like Uncle Warren when I saw him in London."

"Well, he was rather worried when you met him."

"But I didn't like him. He was so serious all the time."

"Yes, but he had a lot to worry him."

Indeed he did have a lot to worry him, and it was his wretched business which was responsible for her present distress, responsible for her fleeing from London, responsible for her leaving William.

As the coach rumbled and jolted on she recalled, as she had recalled a dozen times before, the first time she had seen William. She had been scrubbing the red quarry tiles in the entrance hall of Whitemead Park where she worked as a kitchen maid. She was considering whether to try to get yet more dirt out of the cracks but decided she had done enough. So she began enthusiastically to wash over the area before her with a soaking wet cloth. Then she realised that she had splattered water all over the neat, well-polished boots of a man who was standing before her.

"Oh." She looked up slowly. The boots went up to the knee, and cream trousers went to a narrow-waisted russet brown coat. Then she found she was looking up to the face of an elegant, well-dressed man of about thirty.

"Oh, I be sorry, sir," she said, and began to dry his boots with her apron.

"It does not matter," said the man as he looked down on her, smiling at her confusion. "Just tell your master that I have arrived."

Red-faced, she scrambled to her feet, and ran off to tell Mr Machen.

"Oh dear, it's Lord Lowther," he said. "So soon, and we are not ready for him."

He came out with a show of pleasure and welcomed his guest, enquiring about his journey, asking where he had stopped the previous night, and generally fussing. Hannah stood aside and watched them go into the inner hall. Lord Lowther's servant followed with the luggage.

Hannah got down on her knees again and carried on with her work.

So this was Lord Lowther. Such excitement! Fancy wetting his boots like that! But he was nice, she decided, quite nice. Not like some of the visitors they had. Mrs Turley, the housekeeper, had already told her about him. Mrs Turley was very conscious of her important position in the household. The master respected her opinion, the mistress deferred to her judgment. She was, as she knew, worth her weight in gold. And her weight was considerable. But she manoeuvred her bulk around the house with deliberation and dignity.

"Lord Lowther is a very important person from the Office of Woods in London," she had said. "He is to be a guest here for three days and we all have to make his stay a pleasant one." She had gone on to tell Hannah that while Lord Lowther was with them she was to put on her best black and help in the dining and drawing rooms.

Lord Lowther's presence caused concern and upheaval from Mr Machen downwards. Never had so important a guest stayed at Whitemead Park before. Gentry, yes, but aristocracy, no. The whole house had been thoroughly cleaned from attic to cellar, the special silver was to be used at every meal, and a softer bed for him had been borrowed from relations at English Bicknor.

Lord Lowther, Hannah gathered, had come down from London to advise Mr Machen how to run the Forest of Dean. But he did not need anyone to tell him how to run it. Hannah had heard him telling his wife so at great length only the previous day. Mrs Machen had sighed, and would have shrugged her shoulders if that had not been too great an effort. For Mrs Machen was not a well person. She had an efficient housekeeper in Mrs Turley, and she trusted her to do all that was necessary to ensure that Lord Lowther's stay was a success. Even so, Mrs Machen was finding Lord Lowther's visit too much for her.

The first day of the visit passed tolerably well. Next morning, however, a crisis arose. Lord Lowther's servant, Joseph, was nowhere to be found when his Lordship's morning tea was ready to be taken to him. So Hannah was detailed to take it up.

"And don't forget to knock and wait before you go in," said Mrs Turley.

Hannah duly knocked and waited until she was summoned. She put the tea tray on the table by his bed and went to pull up the blinds.

"Ah, the girl who tried to drown me."

"Yes, I were ever so sorry, sir. You didn't tell Mr Machen, sir, did you?"

"No, of course not."

Hannah waited to be dismissed.

Lord Lowther pulled down the sleeves of his nightshirt. Hannah had never seen such rich fabric, the collar so intricately designed and so delicately stitched. It must be pure silk. She caught his eye and looked away.

"Is it going to be a fine day, do you think?"

"Oh yes, sir," said Hannah, more anxious to please than to give her opinion. She waited.

"What is your name?"

She told him.

"Hannah. Yes, it is an agreeable name." He looked at her as she stood waiting. Then he seemed to lose interest.

"You may go."

She left the room. She had never forgotten how he had lain in the bed with his hands behind his head, appraising her. "Yes, it is an agreeable name. Yes, it is an agreeable name." His voice echoed down the years.

In the afternoon Mrs Turley sent Hannah to get some cream for dinner from the village of Bream, which was about a mile away. It was a fine September day. The leaves on the beech trees were now tipped with rust, though those on the oaks, tardy as ever in response to the seasons, were still green. After a cold start the sun had warmed the earth, and the dew had evaporated and left the grass and trees clean and bright. The world was alive and sparkling.

She walked through the park, and went out by the gate at the other end into the woods. The cream collected, she called for a few minutes on her mother who lived in the village with her unmarried brother, Warren. Warren was not at home, but she exchanged news with her mother and told her about Lord Lowther's visit.

On leaving, she decided that it was such a lovely day that she would steal a few more minutes in the open air before returning by going the long way back to the house. The path ran by the side of a tramroad, and as she approached it she could see a tram with its horse and driver. The reins were slack on the horse's back as it plodded along with firm tread. The driver was smoking his pipe as he walked in harmony alongside his horse. The tram was laden with iron-ore, and was going from the Oakwood mine to the Parkend ironworks.

She loved this walk. It went along a sheltered valley with young oak trees on either side. As she reached the path she disturbed some Forester's sheep, and they plunged into the bracken.

If she had been a man, she mused, she would not have gone into a coal pit like her brothers, or into the ironworks like her uncles. She would have been a tramroad man. What could be more satisfying than leading a horse and tram leisurely through such lovely countryside? But did she really want to be a tram driver? A lot of other jobs would be better. And she was not a man, anyway.

She heard a step and looked back. It was Lord Lowther.

"Hallo - ah, it's Hannah," he said. "I'm lost. Can you show me the way to the house?"

"Of course, your lordship," she said, dropping a curtsy.

They walked along together in silence. She glanced at him sideways, and blushed when she found him looking at her.

"Tell me about yourself, Hannah. How old are you? And how long have you been working for Mr Machen?"

She told him she was 17 and had worked in the house for three months, ever since her father had died. She was lucky to get the job, but she did not like it much. But what was there in the Forest for a girl like her?

"You will get married some day, no doubt."

"Who to, then? To a miner? And have half a dozen kids and be a drudge trying to make ends meet, like my mother did?" She paused and placed a hand on her throat. Such temerity. To speak so freely to a stranger, to a man, and to an aristocrat! She recovered, and gave him a shy smile.

Lord Lowther returned her smile and regarded her curiously. Hannah tried to change the subject.

"But it be a lovely day today, bain't it, sir, and I feels happy." Indeed she felt exhilarated. And then she felt embarrassed, and began to hasten along the footpath. Lord Lowther caught her up.

"What is the hurry?" he said. "You must show me the Forest."

"Yes, sir." They walked side by side.

Silence. Lord Lowther for once in his life was not sure how to handle the situation.

"You like the Forest, I presume. I must confess that I would find permanent residence here boring and would want to return to the delights of London after a short stay. But on a day like today I find the novelty delightful."

"Do that mean, sir," said Hannah doubtfully, "that you don't fancy living 'ere, like?" She thought he was teasing her. But she was not sure. She was nervous.

Lord Lowther tried again. He asked her about her life as a servant at Mr Machen's, and then what her childhood had been. Gradually her nervousness disappeared. She answered his questions at greater and greater length. She told him that none of her family had ever been out of the Forest, but that she had always been curious about life outside.

She was pleased when they arrived back at the house. Lord Lowther went in at the front door; she hurried round to the back. Mrs Turley, who was getting dinner ready, scolded her for taking so long over her errand and told her to peel the potatoes.

She did not see much of him the next day. The day after was Sunday. Over breakfast Lord Lowther shattered the household by announcing that he was enjoying his stay in the Forest so much that unless Mr Machen had any objection he would like to stay on for another two days. Mr Machen, of course, voiced no objection but Hannah, who was serving, could sense his unease and Mrs Machen's near panic at having their guest stay longer than they had expected.

It being Sunday, Mr Machen and Lord Lowther decided that they would go to church for the 11 o'clock service. Mrs Machen announced that she was feeling better today and would join them. Those of the servants who could be spared were, as usual, given time off to go to church also. These included Hannah, so as soon as she had finished her chores she changed her clothes and set out to collect her mother and go to church with her. As she left the house by the back door she passed the library and could hear Lord Lowther politely but firmly telling Mr Machen what he should be doing to improve the growth of the oak trees in the Forest.

Hannah was going up the path towards the woods when she heard the front door of the house close. She glanced back and saw Lord Lowther coming round the corner. She was turning into the woods when she saw him coming up the path. Was he following her? Had he seen her with her cloak and bonnet on as she had passed the library window?

She turned into the woods and slowed her pace a little. He soon caught her up.

"I decided not to go to church after all," he said. "It is such a lovely day that I thought I would go for a walk in this delightful Forest instead. May I accompany you?" Hannah did not reply, but continued along the path.

The day was indeed lovely. The sun was warm, the bees were humming, and a sweet fragrance was in the air. Hannah knew he was glancing sideways at her, and she could imagine a slight smile on his face. They walked in silence for a little. Then they began to chat, he taking the initiative.

After a few minutes he stopped by the side of a large stone, abandoned on the side of the path from a nearby quarry.

"Let us sit down for a minute,' he said.

They sat on the stone and enjoyed the sun. Lord Lowther moved a little closer to her. Hannah edged away, but not too far. She was glad she was wearing her best Sunday clothes.

"I am due to return on Tuesday, you know," he said.

"Yes," said Hannah, "I know. Where do you live in London, sir?"

"In Carlton House Terrace."

"Be your wife there now?"

"What made you think that I am married?"

"Oh, I be sorry."

"There is nothing to be sorry about. No, I am not married."

They both thought for a minute. Suddenly Hannah jumped up.

"I am supposed to be going to church with my mother," she said.

"It would surely be more pleasant to go for a walk with me, would it not?"

"Yes, of course, sir." Hannah smiled, and walked slowly off down the path. He followed. After a few minutes she said. "If we be going for a walk, I suggest we go this way," and she took a narrow path off to the left. Soon they came to the edge of a valley and began to descend. Bracken surrounded them. In the distance a heat haze had risen above a plantation of young oak trees which Hannah knew Mr Machen had supervised the planting of only two years ago, and which were growing sturdy and fast.

They discussed trees, and Hannah felt that she was impressing Lord Lowther with her knowledge. She told him how mice had eaten all Mr Machen's acorns the previous year, and of the severe frost they had endured one May not many years back.

"It was so bad that all the grass in the low parts of the Forest was destroyed," she said. "Not a green leaf left on any oak or beech tree, there wasn't. And the shoots on the trees was all withered."

A squirrel ran across their path, his tail feathery in the wind, and disappeared.

"Where has he gone?"

"Gorn up thic tree," said Hannah, pointing.

"I didn't see him."

"He went up the back. They do always go up the back, so that you don't see where they be going."

"Well, I never knew that," said Lord Lowther. "How clever."

Hannah did not know whether it was clever or not, but she was glad the squirrel had run in front of them. They continued down the hill. Hannah began to run.

"I can't stop. Help!" she laughed.

Lord Lowther ran after her and caught her arm and they fell to the ground. They lay on their backs beside one another and looked up at the sky.

"I have never seen such tall bracken before," he said. "It must be seven feet tall. You call it bracken?" His voice was warm and friendly.

"Bracken or fern," replied Hannah. Then, before she could think, she said, "We do say in the Forest,

If you've never made love in a bed of fern,
Alas, my friend, you've a lot to learn!"

"Well, do you?" he mused; and Hannah opened her eyes and saw his face above hers and smiling at her. Behind him the sunny tips of the bracken moved gently in the breeze.

She became aware of the masculine smell of his clothes, clean, not like the Foresters'. She looked at his grey cravat, and thought of his open neck which she had seen when he was in bed only two days earlier. Then she realised how alone they were, and wondered what he would do. She had been in the bracken with Charley Kear only a fortnight ago. But Charley had no finesse. Worse than that, he did not know what to do. She soon realised that Lord Lowther did. Gently but deliberately he undid the buttons of her blouse and kissed her breast. The kiss went down into her soul, and she felt rich and warm inside. Her heart beat fast, and she lay, waiting. But in spite of the excitement of being made love to by a gentleman, at the back of her mind Hannah realised, coolly and calmly, what she was doing.

That evening at dinner she avoided his eye. As she approached him with the dishes for him to serve himself, she sensed his warmth reaching out to her. Normally she would have listened to the conversation so that she could repeat it to the other servants afterwards, but that evening she heard nothing but a vague burr, even when Lord Lowther was speaking. She was glad when she had finished her duties and was able to go to bed.

The next morning he caught her wrist as they were passing in the upstairs corridor and drew her into his room. He made no reference to the happenings of the previous day, but came straight to the point.

"Would you like to come to London with me?"

Hannah hesitated. "Well, yes sir, of course. Are you offering me a job, like?"

Lord Lowther laughed. "My girl, I am offering you something far, far better than scrubbing steps and peeling potatoes. I am offering you London, the theatre, opera, concerts, pleasure gardens, plenty of clothes, plenty of money with which you can do as you wish."

He looked at her a little shyly. "And I am offering you myself, who I suspect you like a little already and I hope you will like more as time goes on. I want you to come and live with me. I need someone like you to be with me and keep me company - to look after me."

"But you have only known me for a few days, sir." Hannah gazed at him. She liked him, there was no doubt about that, but this was unbelievable. She was about to reject the whole proposal when a small voice at the back of her mind told her that this was her opportunity to get away from the Forest, the opportunity she had always wanted.

"We can tell Mr and Mrs Machen that you are going to be an assistant housekeeper at my London house."

Hannah was silent.

"You will have all you want. Trust me, Hannah. Say 'yes'."

Hannah looked at him. His face was anxious. She could see he badly wanted her to accept his proposition.

"Yes," she said slowly. "I will."

With a relieved smile, he said, "Good." He kissed her on the forehead. "We must leave tomorrow at ten. Can you be ready by then?"

It did not take her long to pack. She had few possessions. She laid out on her bed her best dress, some worsted stockings, a spare pair of shoes, some underwear and a few personal items. Fortunately the other girls who shared the attic with her were busy downstairs. What to put her things in? She moved the old wooden trunk that she used as a locker to the middle of the room and put her possessions in it. The lock was broken, so she secured it with some rope she found in the stables.

Before she went to bed she hurried to her mother's cottage and told her that she was leaving for London in the morning. Her mother looked at her searchingly.

"You've never done no housekeeping. You bain't be going as no housekeeper, I'll be bound."

"This be my big chance, mam. Wish me luck."

"I don't see why thee can't settle down here in the Forest with a nice fellow like Charley Kear. No good can come of thee gallivanting up to London. Still thee would never listen, and I can see thee 'ave made up tha mind."

With this modified blessing, Hannah kissed her mother goodbye.

They left the next morning at ten. Mr Machen had been uncomprehending when he had learnt that he was to lose his kitchen maid at such short notice, but had raised no objection. Nor had Mrs Machen, though the news had done nothing for her health, and she had had to retire to bed.

The luggage was stowed on top of the coach, Hannah's shabby box alongside Lord Lowther's large glistening trunks. Joseph climbed up next to the coachman, and Lord Lowther gave Hannah his hand as she climbed into the coach. As she did so she smiled sweetly at Mrs Turley. Mrs Turley pursed her lips. Assistant housekeeper, indeed.

Hannah came back to the present. That was another coach and another time. The coachman pressed his foot on the brake and drew the reins back hard with a "Whoah." They halted outside the coaching inn at Mitcheldean, a prosperous village on the edge of the Forest.

"We must stop here to change horses," said the fat gentleman.

Hannah was beginning to like him a little. She smiled charitably.

"We have a ten minute wait," he said. "You may wish to get out and stretch your legs."

Hannah thanked him, and she and Charlotte descended. They strolled along the village street in the sunshine, walking past the market hall and on to the church. There they sat on a bench outside. Hannah leaned back with her eyes closed and her face raised to the sun. She relaxed. The sun beat down, penetrating every pore of her skin. For a few seconds, thought, worry, concern were banished. She could see only a bright yellow blank and feel nothing but warmth. She realised how weary she was.

Charlotte positioned herself comfortably and looked around curiously.

"Everything is small here, mamma," she said.

Hannah opened her eyes. "Yes, I suppose so," she said patiently. "You are used to London, where everything is big, too big sometimes. But you will get used to things."

Charlotte grasped her hand. "Look at that girl there, staring at us."

Hannah followed Charlotte's gaze, and saw a small girl standing by the corner of the church. She was about Charlotte's age, but whereas Charlotte was plump and her skin glowed pink, this child was thin and grey. She wore a rough dress and her feet were unshod. The child regarded them with a mixture of awe and suspicion. Hannah recognised her. She was herself at that age - hungry, haggard and dirty.

Her heart went out to the girl. She recalled her own childhood in the Forest,

'They strolled along the village street in the sunshine past the market hall'

how she and her eight brothers and sisters had lived with their parents in a squalid, single-storey squatters' hut on the Forest waste. The stone hut had but one room and was, she remembered, usually damp. She recalled the sight of her father before the fire, washing the grime of the pit from his pitiably thin body while the family busied themselves around him with their own concerns. She remembered how the children snuggled together on frosty nights in the big bed in the corner, piling over them coats and shawls to protect them from the chilly draughts from under the door. For before dawn put forth its grey fingers, the fire died down and the room grew cold. She recaptured the noise of water lashing on the turf roof when it rained and, if it rained long enough, the incessant drip-drip-drip of water from the roof into the room. Above all she remembered being hungry, oh so hungry, with a gnawing ache in the stomach that rarely seemed to go away.

But then, Hannah concluded, life had been much the same for all squatter families in the Forest. Indeed their nearest neighbours, the Morses, who lived 200 yards away in a similar hut to theirs, were in a worse plight, for the breadwinner had been injured in the pit and walked about with a twisted hip and a painful limp.

There had been some happier times, of course, some lighter moments. She recalled sitting under the trees in the summer sunshine playing with her siblings, rolling in the undergrowth, throwing last year's acorns at one another; and winter evenings when the family sat warm and snug round the fire - for whatever they lacked, they had plenty of coal and wood to keep themselves warm. She saw again the bright red glow from the coals, the yellow shooting flames and sparking fireworks from the wood, and the beautiful warmth that reached out to them all.

It was at such times that she would be content, lying with Warren at her side, whispering and fidgeting and telling secrets. Thoughts of her comradeship with Warren reminded her of the kindness of her father and the occasional demonstration of love from her mother. But this was rare. Her mother may have had an infinite amount of love for all her children, but she had time to give no more than a small faction of her attention to each of them.

Hannah's thoughts turned to an incident that had caused the family their greatest hardship. One winter her father, like the other Forest miners, could not sell his coal. Imported coal from the north, it was said, was selling more cheaply than Forest coal in the markets. Hunger was soon upon them, real, stark, gnawing hunger. The chickens and the pig that used to graze among the trees had all been killed and eaten. The weather was freezing and the children were unwilling to go out in the snow in their ragged, worn-out garments. Faces became gaunt and grey, eyes began to search nervously everywhere all the time for something to eat.

Hannah's father had been approached with a proposition by some fellow miners who were also at their wits end for food for their families. The idea was to fell a Forest tree, a fine broad-limbed oak that belonged to the Crown, and take it in a cart belonging to one of them to sell in Lydney. Fearing that he would be caught, her mother had urged her father not to take part in the venture. They had argued, face to face, shouting at each other, her father's voice forceful and loud, her mother's frightened and strangely high-pitched. The smaller children, wild-eyed and bewildered, had clung to one another in the corner of the room, not understanding the reason for their parents' passion. The older children, including Hannah and Warren, had stood in another group. They understood and supported their father.

Hannah flinched now as she remembered how her father had pushed her mother aside so that she fell to the ground, and with an oath had stormed out of the hut to join the other men. They went deep into the woods, and with much exertion felled the tree, trimmed its branches and were loading the trunk onto the cart when several Forest keepers appeared. There was a fight, and her father and his friends were arrested and taken away. The next day they were brought before the local magistrate and sentenced to four months in Littledean gaol.

The family were now left without a breadwinner. Shortly they heard that the coal market had improved and Forest coal could once again be sold in Lydney. Warren, who was about ten at this time and the oldest of the boys, had already been working with his father in the pit. He maintained that he knew enough about mining to carry on in his father's place, and decided to do so. He did not open up the pit and work it alone; they all went down. But even with the help of their mother and the other children - even the four year old helped - they hardly produced as much as the father could dig on his own. Hannah remembered how she had donned a harness, got down on her hands and knees and pulled a truck of coal. The chain had chafed her thighs as it passed between her legs, and she remembered, even now, how the pin-point of the daylight at the end of the tunnel remained small for so long as she crawled through the mud dragging the truck behind her towards it.

When they had dug sufficient coal to fill a cart, they pushed it down to Lydney to see what it would fetch.

"Two shillings the lot," said the dealer.

"Two shillings!" said Warren. "That's a week's work for us.'

"Take it or leave it," said the dealer. They took it.

That day Warren became a man. That day he learned how the world could be unjust and cruel. That day, as he later told her, he determined he was going to do something about the conditions under which Forest miners worked and the poverty they endured.

Warren had seen that he would never succeed in his aim without becoming literate. Their father had taught both Warren and herself to read and write, but they could do so only haltingly, and their reading material was confined to the one book the house possessed, the Bible. Warren was determined to read as well as educated people. It was a daunting task. Every spare minute he could find from his work in the pit he spent reading. In daylight in the summer, and by the light of a solitary candle in the winter he read and read. A schoolmaster in Bream encouraged him to continue to educate himself, and lent him books.

Gradually, Warren's reading widened. He learnt about the rights of the free miners in the Forest and how they had been granted to his ancestors centuries earlier. And he learnt how those rights were being stolen by the hard businessmen from outside the Forest - foreigners they called them - who were buying up the coal pits from the free miners and depriving them of their livelihood.

Hannah's reaction to the hardships suffered by the Foresters had been quite different from Warren's. While she regarded the conditions in which she and her family lived as unbearable, she could not see that anything could be done to change them. The only thing to do was to get out.

This she did at the first opportunity. She had heard that Mrs Machen was looking for a girl to help in the house, and went round and knocked on the kitchen door. A doubtful Mrs Turley interviewed her and took her on as a kitchen maid. The work was hard, and the discipline strict. She resented Mrs Turley's tyranny. The two other serving girls, however, were friendly, though they could not replace the close warmth of her brothers and sisters.

She soon grew used to her new life. When there was no-one about she could survey the hitherto unknown world of how the rich lived. To her the Machens were rich beyond belief. When she went home on her half day off, she would tell her mother how they had more food than they could eat, more clothes than they could wear, carpets on the floor and a dozen candles burning at a time in the drawing room. With three reasonable meals a day and pocket money of a shilling a week, she blossomed. Her body rounded, and she attained the full physical beauty of a woman.

The girl had left the corner of the church and was coming nearer. Hannah took a sixpence from her purse and offered it to her. The child looked at her for a second and then, seizing the money, ran off without a word.

"Why did you give her sixpence mamma?" asked Charlotte.

"I was sorry for her. She looked so hungry and poor."

"Yes," said Charlotte, "but I didn't like her, though."

"Very often one tends not to like people one is sorry for."

Hannah rose. "Come, we must get back. The horses will have been changed by now."

When they returned they found that not only had the horses been changed but two more had been attached at the front to get the coach to the top of Plump Hill.

Charlotte was intrigued by the climb up the hill. The horses sweated and strained, and every yard revealed a wider view. The young men on the top of the coach enjoyed it too, urging the coachman to lay on his whip more generously lest they all went backwards.

At the top the coach stopped, and Hannah and Charlotte got out for a few minutes while the men unharnessed the extra horses to take them back to Mitcheldean. By the roadside was a steep drop to a small valley. Hannah looked down at some cottages nestling isolated at the bottom. What sort of people lived there, she wondered. Were they happy?

In the distance she could see the River Severn, curving like a snake and sparkling in the morning sun. Beyond the river was the blurred horizon where cloud and land mingled. All was still. She twisted on her heels so that she could take in everything in one sweep. Between the valley at her feet and the river were gentle hills, softened by trees. Trees were in fact everywhere, oaks mainly, but there were a few beech and elm here and there, all looking strong and healthy. Young trees they were, for the most part. This was Mr Machen's work. This was the work he had been appointed at Whitemead Park to do, to fill in the large brown areas by planting new young trees in their thousands. The Forest - her Forest - lay before her. Why *her* Forest? she wondered. Why had she thought that? Was she glad to be back?

She and Charlotte climbed back in, and the coach started again on its journey to Coleford. It crunched the stones on the road as it gradually got up speed, and then maintained a steady, rocking motion. Hannah lowered the window and gripped the ledge with both hands. As she gazed out, the breeze gently ruffled her hair and caressed her cheek, heightening her colour.

She had come back to the Forest because she wanted to leave London, and Dean was the only other place she knew. Oh, the contrast! Contrast in all ways, the poverty of the Forest and the riches of Mayfair, the beauty of the Forest and the ugliness and squalor of parts of Westminster. Yet the poor in the Forest were surely not as badly off as the poor in London. In the smelly back alleys of Westminster there was never light or fresh air. In the Forest, even if one had an empty belly, one could always sit in the sun and breathe air that no-one had ever breathed before.

"I'm tired," announced Charlotte. "How long will it be before we get to Coleford, mamma?"

"In less than an hour, I think. I should have a little sleep if I were you, and then you will be fresh when we arrive."

"Yes," said Charlotte, and she snuggled up against her mother.

Hannah looked down at her child. She recalled how she, too, had been tired when she had reached this spot ten years ago. But she had been going in the other direction, on her way to London with Lord Lowther. Her excitement at escaping from the Forest had deprived her of all sleep the previous night, and she had dozed and Lord Lowther had put his arm around her to protect her from the jolts of his coach. For though it was an excellent coach, and well sprung with all the latest inventions, the roads had been rougher then than they were now, and travelling was hard. With his arm around her she had gradually fallen into a deep sleep, and had not wakened up until they reached Oxford. Here they had stopped and put up at an inn.

They had stayed in Oxford for two days. Lord Lowther had some business there, but his main purpose in stopping was to equip Hannah with some better clothes. He had not expected much from the shops in the town, but even the best of them did not come up to his lowered expectations.

"Never mind," he said. "We will get some things that will serve until we get to London."

In the first shop Lord Lowther sat near the dressing room on a chair that one of the assistants, obviously impressed, had hastened to bring for him. He sat smoking a long pipe, one leg crossed elegantly over the other, his stick in one hand. He explained to the assistants what clothing Hannah required, and commented on the various dresses she wore as she emerged from the dressing room. She listened in awe to his comments, and was impressed by the fact that he knew exactly what he wanted.

Though the assistants gazed with wide, reverend eyes at Lord Lowther, they were no more than coolly polite to Hannah. Her bearing and the clothes she had arrived in fell far short of what they expected from the companion of a person as distinguished as a lord. For her part, Hannah was too intrigued by what was going on to notice their reactions. Beautiful clothes they all were, clothes that she had never seen the likes of and had never dreamed she would wear. Underclothes as well. Silk. She was amused at the little rolls of material that the assistants advised her to put under her breasts to make them more prominent. What ideas these people had! But she was not averse to trying the rolls, and was relieved when they stayed in place. The dresses she decided were extremely low cut, but she accepted that this was upper class fashion.

"You must wear these clothes as if you have always been used to them," Lord Lowther had told her.

Then they went to a shoe shop. Lord Lowther waited patiently while assistants ran around with boxes piled high. It was while she was trying on a pair of soft leather shoes - so ridiculously slight that at home they would be in tatters before she reached the pig-sty - that she realised, fully, just what Lord Lowther proposed for her. There had been no discussion on the role she to assume. He had decided.

"I think we are going to get along very well together," he said as an assistant loaded the shoes into the carriage, "don't you?"

"Yes, sir," she replied.

He looked at her with amusement, and said "I think you had better not call me 'sir'. What about 'William'?" He smiled.

She smiled back, and clutched his arm. He *was* a kind man, and considerate. And, she thought - dare she think it? - he was in love with her. Or was he just infatuated, or even worse, did he just need a mistress on hand to satisfy his physical needs? No, she decided, he loved her, as she loved him.

They arrived in London at Carlton House Terrace in the early evening. The housekeeper, Mrs Beale, met them in the hall. She was a neat, compact, middle-aged little woman, dressed entirely in black. Her bird-like face bore a faint and permanent smile. She always held her hands together before her, and leaned forward slightly from the waist, as if to be certain to catch every hint, every nuance.

Mrs Beale had obviously been informed about Hannah's arrival and what position she was to hold in the house.

"This is Mrs James," William said briefly. "She will be staying with us." That was all.

Hannah smiled timidly at Mrs Beale, and was half inclined to drop a curtsy. Meanwhile Mrs Beale had dropped a deep one, and was now looking at her steadily and inquiringly.

"Mrs James will occupy the annexe," said William.

"Yes, my lord."

The annexe, Hannah soon discovered, was a small house next to Lord Lowther's. It was nominally a separate establishment, but there were communicating doors on every floor which were never locked, and the place was serviced by servants from the big house. Hannah found it fully furnished and equipped. Her bedroom, a large room decorated in pink and white, overlooked

St. James's Park. There were two other bedrooms and a sitting room. There was also a dining room, a study, a kitchen and servants' quarters.

Hannah walked round, examining every corner of every room. All was bright and clean. She gently touched the vases of flowers on the side tables, marvelled at the old lantern clock on the mantelpiece, enjoyed the feel of the satin on the chairs, and wondered whose job it was to produce such a high polish on the floors.

So this is a small house, thought Hannah. To her it was wonderfully large, but she conceded that it was small compared with Lord Lowther's mansion next door. This, then, was to be her home, her own establishment, as William called it.

"Have the whole place re-decorated as you wish," he told her. She was satisfied with the decorations as they were, but later had them changed because he clearly wished it. She changed the pink in the bedroom to light green to remind her of the Forest.

Later that evening she donned the silk off-the-shoulder gown that William had bought for her at Oxford, and went down for supper. At the bottom of the stairway she stood uncertainly in the hall. William came out of his study on the left and escorted her into the sitting room. The evening was chilly, and a fire had been lit.

"You look charming, my dear," he said. "But we'll get you some more clothes in a day or two. I have a good friend who will introduce you to the best shops and advise you generally."

Williams pulled a cord to summon a servant to mend the fire. Hannah could not see that it needed attention, apart from a few pokes that she would willingly have given it herself. But as the thought came to her, her attention was taken by the fireplace itelf.

Its stately proportions made the large fire seem small. Seeing her reaction, William told her that it had been carved from Tuscan marble especially imported by his grandfather. Hannah touched the marble and commented on its polish.

"Rather than a polish," William said, "I think it has a glow that springs from within. It seems to exude the warmth of Italy whence it came."

Hannah scarcely understood, but her reaction was straight and simple. "Oh, it be beautiful," she said. "I 'ave never seen anything so lovely before in my life."

She turned her attention to the chairs and settees. They were covered with striped satin of mauve and white with just a thread of gold. So delicate were they that they made Mr Machen's windsor chairs, which she had so admired, seem crude. The chairs were Sheraton, William told her, Sheraton had designed them especially to go with the room. He did not like modern furniture, he said, and would not have them replaced.

Hannah went over to the curtains, now drawn. They were mauve, and crowned by looped and generously folded pelmets, and fell with a sweep from ceiling to floor. The wallpaper, she learned, was Chinese and hand-painted. The ceiling was high yet in perfect proportion. Against a blue background, cornices and stucco decorations were picked out in gold. The carpet, which spread over most of the floor, leaving only an edge of polished oak, was blue with gold decoration. William pointed out to her that the pattern on the ceiling was repeated in the carpet.

The whole room was lit by a hundred candles in an enormous candelabra hanging from the encrusted centre of the ceiling. The shimmer of blue and gold overwhelmed Hannah, and she wondered whether she would ever sit comfortably in such a room.

"And here, to make you even more beautiful than you are, is a necklace. It was the best Oxford could supply. They had not a great selection there, but it will serve you for a few days."

He placed it round her neck, and kissed her. Hannah thanked him, and looked at it in a mirror. The candles on each side of the frame flickered and caused it to gleam. Hannah's eyes moistened. The necklace was simple in design, but of gold. William might not think much of it, but to her it would always mean a lot. It was his first gift of jewellery to her.

At first Hannah, being a practical woman, had fears about running the enormous establishment that William called his home. She was, however, soon reassured. Mrs Beale ran everything and received the necessary money direct from William's secretary. Though Hannah came into contact with Mrs Beale almost every day, she left all the household decisions, even the menus, to her.

Hannah did not like her. Perhaps she reminded her of Mrs Turley of Whitemead Park. Anyway, she knew that in her calculating, mincing way, Mrs Beale was hostile. To tell the truth, Hannah was a little frightened of her. But Mrs Beale did her no harm, was polite and always helpful; and Hannah was careful never to upset her.

Hannah had her own allowance to spend on herself. At first it seemed enormous, but she soon found that she had to spend lavishly to keep herself clothed in the manner William expected. However, she did not waste money, and prudently put some of the allowance aside in a bank account she opened for the purpose.

The first afternoon after her arrival at Carlton House Terrace, while she was still marvelling at the contents of her house and her new world, William sent word that he would like to see her in the sitting room. She entered rather nervously. William was sitting in an armchair by the window chatting to an elegant woman of about 40, who was seated on a settee. Hannah noted her poise, the elegance of her wine-red gown and her discreet make-up.

"Come in, Hannah, and let me introduce you to a good friend of mine, the

Honourable Mrs Dawson Damer."

Hannah dropped a curtsy.

"Come over and sit by me, my dear," said Mrs Dawson Damer. She patted the settee, and Hannah noticed that as she sat down Mrs Dawson Damer's eyes went quickly over her, taking her measure in a second. Hannah was a little disconcerted at the quick appraisal the lady gave her, but soon warmed to her. This, then, was the good friend William had said would help her settle down in his world.

After a few minutes of general conversation, William rose. "I must go now," he said.

"Oh, no," pleaded Hannah.

"Oh yes," he replied teasingly. "I'll ring and you can order tea."

"So you come from the country," said Mrs Dawson Damer.

"Yes, the Forest of Dean. It is in Gloucestershire." She pronounced it 'Glahstersher'.

Mrs Dawson Damer did not recognise the place at first. Then she nodded. "Oh yes. Gloucestershire." But she clearly had not heard of the Forest of Dean.

"I am sure it must be very lovely there. I hope you like it in London. You will soon settle down. But you must learn to do things correctly. Do not hesitate to ask me. I want to help you."

She looked at Hannah, and then smiled. "You will manage, I can see that."

They continued to chat about generalities, Mrs Dawson Damer doing most of the talking.

"Look, I must go now. But come round to see me on Thursday afternoon about three o'clock. Come by carriage, of course." She rose. "Yes, wear that dress. It suits you."

The first visit to Mrs Dawson Damer's establishment in Montpelier Square was a success. The two women clearly liked each other, and Hannah often went to see her. More and more Mrs Dawson Damer offered Hannah advice on her role as William's mistress. She told Hannah about William's background.

"His father is the second Earl of Lonsdale and his mother is Augusta, the daughter of the ninth Earl of Westmorland. He is without doubt the aristocrat of aristocrats, my dear."

Hannah smiled.

"And he is a charming man. I have known him since he was a boy, and I am very fond of him. He has always been charming - but I must warn you, he uses his charm to get his way. Suddenly you find he's got what he wanted, and you didn't know! But you can't be cross with him. Anyway, you will find out all about him in time."

Mrs Dawson Damer then described the Lonsdale estates that Lord Lowther would inherit on his father's death.

"But he told me that he already has lots of land up in Westmorland."

"Yes he has, but he will inherit more in due course. And he is already very, very wealthy. He goes up to Westmorland several times a year to his estates. I am told that he's a very good landlord, and spends vast sums of money on drainage. It is supposed to grow better crops, I think, but I don't claim to understand it."

Mrs Dawson Damer then turned to more important matters. "You must not expect to have many women friends," she said. "Of course the golden age of mistresses - if you can call it that - has gone, but there are still many around -discreetly around, naturally. And always will be, I suppose. Now before the wars with the French, it was the fashion for single young men to keep mistresses, and quite a few married ones did as well. It was *de rigeur.* The Prince of Wales had his Mrs Fitzherbert, although he was in fact secretly married to her. A lot of people don't know that."

Hannah had never heard of Mrs Fitzherbert, but was intrigued by Mrs Dawson Damer's revelations.

"Then there were his brothers. The Duke of Sussex had his charming aristocratic Cecilia, the Duke of York his cockney girl from Bowling Alley, the Duke of Kent his French piece - 27 years that liaison lasted, until they made him marry - and the Duke of Clarence had Mrs Jordan. She had been a comedy actress, you know, and they say she was very good, too."

"Do they?" breathed Hannah.

"All the Royal Dukes had their mistresses and did not care who knew it. Then for various reasons they gave them up. But they all made good provison for them. Except the Duke of York. He just threw Mary Ann out. There was terrible scandal. But the Prince of Wales provided well for Mrs Fitzherbert when they parted. They were together for twenty-five years, you know, and split up because he had to get married to provide an heir to the throne. And there were other women as well. But they always loved each other, though they had some mighty rows in their time."

Hannah smiled inwardly as she wondered whether William would follow the Duke of York and cast her off without a penny, or the Prince of Wales and provide for her. She glanced at Mrs Dawson Damer, but the good lady was lost in a reverie. Then she looked up and smiled.

"She is still alive, you know, Mrs Fitzherbert. She is a kindly soul."

Hannah later learnt that Mrs Dawson Damer was Mrs Fitzherbert's adopted daughter.

Mrs Dawson Damer changed the subject. "Well, now that you are under the protection of Lord Lowther we must see that you conduct yourself with dignity and reticence, and that he continues to love you."

Hannah liked the expression 'under the protection of Lord Lowther'. It conveyed the situation elegantly but with unmistakable clarity.

Later, in her room, Hannah pondered on her conversation with Mrs Dawson Damer. She wondered whether the lady had been someone's mistress.

There was certainly no mention of a Mr Dawson Damer; but she was comfortably off and knew her way round society. Hannah soon thought of her as 'Mrs D D'.

Under her expert guidance Hannah's gaucheness disappeared. During one afternoon visit to her house Hannah was introduced to two of her friends. With her perfect judgment Mrs Dawson Damer had chosen women who quickly put Hannah at her ease. The meeting made Hannah more confident. From being apprehensive about her status, she soon began to find her way confidently around the limited society she could move in. The important thing for the mistress of a public person, as she learnt from her new friend, was to recognise the dividing line between public and private life.

William also helped to equip her for her new position. He arranged for her to have lessons in elocution, music and dancing. She was determined to make him satisfied with her in all ways, and was a willing learner. "I do not want you to lose your Forest accent," he said, "but perhaps London grammar instead of Gloucestershire grammar?" She agreed, and they both laughed. And soon she was speaking like a London aristocrat, although she never quite lost her Forest accent.

Her elocution teacher found she was a good pupil, and wanted to learn more about books and reading in general. He encouraged her to build on the small ability to read that she had acquired from her father, and she was soon reading widely. She examined every leather-bound volume in William's extensive library, but found them dull. So she visited the bookshops in Piccadilly and at Charing Cross. Her favourite was a little shop near St. Martin in the Field, and she placed a permanent order with the old bookseller there for all the new novels as they came out.

For knowledge of what was going on in a wider world than she had ever believed could exist, she was soon going through *The Times* every day. This, she decided with satisfaction, was no small feat, considering its small print and long words. Her favourite place for reading was in her sitting room, in the bay of a window that overlooked the park; and she went there every morning after breakfast. Reading by candle light, she thought, was bad for the sight. Ten candles, even a hundred backed by a big mirror, were no substitute for good, honest daylight.

She enjoyed her dancing lessons, and was intrigued by the tiny fiddle the dancing master played to give a tune for their steps. She loved all the dances he taught her, but especially the waltz and the Sir Roger de Coverley.

"A generation ago the waltz was not considered a suitable dance for young ladies," he told her. "But it is quite acceptable now, though there are still some ladies of more mature years who will not dance it."

A singing master came to give her lessons twice a week. He improved her singing voice and, incidentally, her speaking voice, which acquired a deeper, firmer timbre. She also began piano lessons, but it soon became apparent that she had no aptitude for the instrument and she dropped them.

Every day her knowledge grew, her abilities increased and her powers of thought were refined and developed. Lessons took up only a few hours a day, and she arranged them at times when William was engaged elsewhere. The remainder of the day she usually spent with him. She was aware that he was pleased with the way she was developing, and his approval gave her confidence.

However, she soon realised that she was attractive not only to William but to other men. A glance from a stranger in the street or a friend of William's who came to the house confirmed this. She was pleased, but at the same time frightened about it. However, she quickly learnt to erect a barrier of coolness -oh, ever so charmingly - when she suspected it was necessary. There was never any problem for her, she realised, because not once since she had come to live with William had she conceived an interest in another man.

Yet in spite of her growing confidence, she knew that in her position she could never be accepted as a full member of society. Free and easy as upper class morals were in England in the early 19th century before Victoria imposed a morality that was to last a hundred years, the line of demarcation that separated a mistress from a wife was inexorable and could not be crossed. She accepted the situation, although guided by William she ventured into some public areas. And, of course, she went with him to the theatre and to the public entertainments at Ranalagh and Vauxhall Gardens, with their music and punch and judy shows and performing bears.

Just occasionally she was lonely, not so much for people, but for somewhere she could wholeheartedly belong. One day, as she sat by the sitting room window and looked over the park, she realised that she was lonely for the Forest, with its trees shimmering in the sunlight, the long, cool walks with the dappled shadows on the path, the foxgloves and bluebells in the spring and the bracken in the summer, the fresh breezes that blew from the Severn, the hot sunny days and the cool fresh mornings.

But the mood passed when William came in, and they were together again. She ran to him and sat on his knee, and swung her legs as she snuggled against him. Distinctive was the smell of his clean linen with the faint odour of his lemon and vanilla perfume. He ruffled her dark curls and ran his finger down the curve of her forehead, and she felt him kiss the nape of her neck. She appealed to him, she knew, whether she was serious or merry, talkative or silent. Her simple love for him itself made him love her the more.

Hannah mingled freely with William's friends when they visited the house. It was William's wish. On such occasions she could see how proud he was to have her present. When the men were not in the billiard room they would sometimes join her round the fire, and chat and drink. She would sit on the side, joining in the conversation occasionally, and doing embroidery. This was another social grace she had acquired, though the embroidery she produced she willingly admitted was uneven and ragged. But Williams loved to see her doing it, and she was happy because he was pleased. Occasionally she would join them at the card table and gamble at loo, but she always lost.

One evening while sitting with William and his friends and listening to their conversation she realised with surprise that, underneath their charm, urbanity and superficial wit, his friends were no more intelligent than she was. She could see the thrust of William's arguments when they could not; she could immediately present the appropriate response when they did not take William's point. But in such cases she joined in with care, for her instinct told her that a clever woman was too astute to show her cleverness.

When the guests had gone she would sit quietly with William and talk over the day's happenings. She could then say precisely what she thought. William appreciated such moments, and she felt an intellectual kinship with him that she had never felt with anyone else. Afterwards, as they snuggled up in bed, the intellectual togetherness transmuted hitself into a physical relationship that bound them even closer. And after they had been together and she lay in his arms, she felt a peace that she had never experienced before.

Hannah soon learnt of the important place politics had in William's life, a passion that had been with him since his teens. His father, Lord Lonsdale, had encouraged him, since he believed that the aristocracy was meant to run the country.

"Of course, he was right. All this Whig talk about widening the franchise is rubbish," William would say. "You cannot expect people busy in trade and industry to govern the country well. The aristocracy must rule - we have been doing it successfully in this country for centuries - but you have to go about it in the right way. You must not encourage excesses like the ones that led to the French Revolution. But then the French aristocracy had no sense of duty.

"My father promised me that I should become a member of parliament when I became of age," he went on, "and true to his word he bought me the seat for Cockermouth. I was in the House of Commons shortly after my 21st birthday. Within a few years I was junior Lord of the Admiralty, and then I was appointed Commissioner for Indian Affairs. A couple of years ago I was made First Commissioner of Woods and Forests." He laughed. "If I had not been, I should not have gone down to the Forest of Dean, and I would not have met you."

Hannah reached out and held his hand. "Dear William," she said simply, "I am so glad you did. But you had no desire to do anything else but go into politics?" she asked.

"No, I went into politics because I wanted that above all else. I always get what I want. If I had wanted to go into the church, I would have become a rector somewhere on one of my father's estates, and been a bishop by now, I shouldn't wonder. But I left the cloth to my younger brother. A pulpit suits him. Had I wanted to become a sailor I would have taken a commission in the navy, and would have been an admiral by now. But I alway wanted to go into politics and though I am not prime minister yet, I still have hopes."

Hannah pondered whether William was so assured because he was certain of his own abilities or because he believed that his family's wealth and position would achieve his aim. She was immediately ashamed of such disloyal thoughts, and decided that it was the former. As he talked on she settled back in her corner of the settee and concluded that he had, as far as she could judge, all the attributes of a successful politician. As well as being educated, knowledgeable, and incapable of being ruffled, he was charming, even-tempered, shrewd and capable of making a quick decision when the need arose. At least those were her conclusions. His ability to make quick decisions, he once assured her, almost always resulted in right ones, though he cheerfully admitted that they occasionally were tragically wrong. He had made a quick decision about her, Hannah remembered but, so far at least, he clearly did not consider that he had made a mistake.

As a member of parliament William would go down to the House when it was sitting; but such attendances did not take up much of his time. The House, Hannah learnt, sat for only a few months in the year and daily sittings did not begin until late afternoon. Discussions about politics, however, went on all the time. Not a day went by when he did not meet other members of parliament or other government ministers or friends to discuss the latest developments. Politics was his life, and the heart of his ambition.

She encouraged him to talk about his job as First Commissioner of Woods. Every Tuesday and Thursday mornings he went down to Whitehall to the Office of Woods, arriving punctually at eleven. With his two junior ministers he would sit at the large oak table in his room overlooking the river and decide how the various Royal Forests and establishments under his control should be run.

His secretary would read out the letters he had received from the deputy surveyors of the different Forests, and after discussing their problems with the other Commissioners William would instruct the reply to be sent.

One of the deputy surveyors was, of course, Edward Machen, and knowing of her interest, William often told Hannah what was going on in the Forest of Dean. "He is a very competent fellow, is Machen," he once said. "I wish they were all as conscientious as he is."

Hannah enjoyed these conversations with William, whether they were about the Forest of Dean and Mr Machen, or about other places or people they knew. William was ready to answer any questions she asked, although she was always careful not to pry into matters that did not concern her. There were also questions she would dearly have loved to ask which did concern her. Did William, for example, have a wife with whom he did not live? Had he had other mistresses before her? If so, what had happened to them? And then arose the further question that no-one could answer. What would happen to her? In the happiness of the present she suppressed this question about the future.

William's official duties left him plenty of spare time. He devoted much of it to horses. He had a stud near Epsom, and his aim was one day to win the Derby. He also had a stable at the back of Carlton House Terrace, and every day he and Hannah would go riding in Hyde Park. Hannah shared his love of horses. Many a time she had ridden bareback in the Forest, and she soon became a good orthodox rider, thought she disliked riding side-saddle. On fine days they would go farther afield into the countryside at Edgware, stopping for refreshment at village inns. These were the days that Hannah loved most, cantering along at William's side, going wherever the whim took them, with no-one in the world knowing where they were.

It was on return from a ride in Hyde Park that Hannah realised that she was pregnant. She did not tell William for some weeks, being apprehensive about his reaction. When she did tell him, to her relief he did not seem to mind. Indeed he seemed pleased, and was patient and sympathetic during the pregnancy.

The baby, a healthy girl, was baptised in a small church in Soho. The ceremony was simple. 'Charlotte James' was entered in the baptismal book, with John James entered in the column reserved for the name of the child's father. William had seen to this, and Hannah's child was spared the usual description of 'base born' or 'bastard'.

On William's orders a nursery and quarters for a nurse and servant who were to look after the baby had been prepared in the annexe. The baby lived there, and life in the main house proceeded as if there were no child about at all.

Hannah spent all the time she could with Charlotte. When William went out she usually hurried to the nursery and stayed there until he came back. She wished - oh, she wished - that he would accept the child and invite her to bring her into the main house, but he only occasionally asked after her and, when Hannah replied, said 'Good', nodded his head, and went on to talk about something else.

Once when Charlotte was about two years old, Hannah returned from a visit to her bookshop near St. Martin in the Field, and entered, as she often did, by the main house door instead of her own front door. She found Charlotte happily running round the hall with William in attendance. As William explained, he had entered the hall from his study a few minutes before to hear a quiet bump-bump-bump from the staircase and was surprised to see young Charlotte systematically descending the Adam staircase feet first on her front. She must have come through the annexe door on the second floor and, since she was quite incapable of walking downstairs in the normal way, had slid all the way down the staircase to the hall. When she had reached the bottom she had stood up unsteadily and looked at William. Nonplussed he had got down on his haunches and held his arms out to her. She gurgled with delight and ran towards him, and then, just as she was within a foot of his outstretched arms, gurgled again and veeered round towards the front door. Just then Hannah entered. Seeing her mother, Charlotte squeaked joyously and fell into her arms. A few seconds later a distraught nurse came hurrying down the stairs and, with scared eyes and muttered apologies, retrieved the baby.

William had seemed amused at the incident and from then on had occasionally suggested that Hannah should bring Charlotte downstairs. But the relationship did not develop. Charlotte never again demonstrated that spontaneous, loving approach to William that she had shown when they had met in the hall, and had never again intrigued and fascinated him as she had done on that first occasion.

The situation worried her and gradually attracted other concerns which coalesced to form a single question that now came to her repeatedly when she was sitting quietly in her room or walking with Charlotte in the park; what would become of her in the end? Dare she hope that her present position would continue until old age and death? Would Williams give her up if he became prime minister?

When she had come up from the Forest, so simple and trusting, she had only a vague idea of what she wanted from life, and could not formulate positive ideas, only express vague yearnings. In truth, she had had a better idea of what she did *not* want, and that had guided her actions. In those days she had been willing just to be William's mistress. Now, however, she had Charlotte, and her thoughts were turning towards marriage. This legal stamp on their relationship would give her the final security in society that she wanted. But mistresses seldom married their men, and it was clear that, much as he loved her, William would not marry her. Moreover, she could not see herself accepted by William's aristocratic family. She had long suspected that old Lord Lonsdale had refused to receive her, and that was why William went north to visit his parents alone.

All this saddened her; but she tried to accept that nothing could be done. God had, after all, given her so much - a comfortable existence in a new and exciting world, Charlotte and William to love and cherish, and William's love and protection. But her fears came back again and again.

The coach lumbered on, and Hannah was aroused from her reverie. Charlotte was now awake and gazing out of the window at the trees and the cottages on the Forest waste, and especially at the Foresters as they went by with their horses and donkeys laden high with wood and coal. They passed a young man and woman on foot, poorly dressed but vibrant with life. The young man threw back his head as he smiled broadly at Charlotte. His face, she could see, was whisker-free and his skin was smooth and clean and rosy. The young woman was fresh-eyed and darker than the man. She had a basket on her hip and clutched her skirt with her free hand. She also smiled. Charlotte leaned out as the coach passed them, and the young man waved vigorously, holding his arm up high. Then, with a twinkle, they turned and were gone. What lovely people, Charlotte thought. She might enjoy living in the Forest.

The coach began to descend a hill.

"Where are we now?" she asked.

"Over there is Harry Hill."

Charlotte smiled mischievously. "Is he the brother of May Hill?" she said. Hannah put her arm around her and hugged her. They smiled at each other conspiratorially.

"And you see that church?" said Hannah. "I went there once with Uncle Warren to a wedding of a cousin of ours."

While Charlotte looked at the church, Hannah thought about Warren. He was a great man for religion. Twice to church on Sundays. You would not think a man with such wild ideas would have any time for real religion. She herself went to church, of course, everyone did. But Warren was serious about it. He was too intense.

"You be too intense about everything, Warren," she had once said. "Don't matter what it is, miners' rights, miners' wages - or religion."

"They be connected," he had replied. "God didn't never intend for us Foresters to live like we do, and no-one's going to tell me He did. Why can't we get a better share of the profits for our work? It's us miners that win the coal from the ground, not them masters, them foreigners who come into the Forest and take over our pits and then give us jobs on their terms."

Hannah brushed remembrance of this particular speech of Warren's aside; she had heard it all so many times. Even so, as she sat next to Charlotte on her way back to the Forest she could not think of anyone or anything but Warren. She remembered that day last year when she received a letter from him. This had never happened before. Even Foresters who had learnt to write did not write letters except in special circumstances. The maid had brought it to her with her breakfast tray. The letter was brief, and she could see how slowly and with what effort Warren had written it. He was coming up to London on business the week after next, he said. Since he had not been there before he wondered if she could find him somewhere to stay.

Hannah thought. He could not stay with her, that was clear. But she could arrange for him to stop at some lodgings. She wrote back to say that she would arrange for him to stay at the Tun Inn in Fleet Street where the coaches from Gloucester stopped. She would meet him if he would tell her the time he would arrive.

A week later Warren wrote again, stating the day he was coming and the time the Gloucester coach was due to arrive. A few minutes before it was due, Hannah's carriage swept into Fleet Street. It drove down the middle of the road with a flourish. The coachman cracked his whip at some ragged boys who did not move quickly enough for him, and the coach splatted mud over everyone. Twenty yards before it reached the Tun Inn Hannah ordered the coachman to draw to the side. She had only a short time to wait before the Gloucester coach turned into the inn yard. She told her coachman to wait for her, and went to the inn.

When she saw Warren climbing down from the coach roof, she ran to greet him. The last few years had disappeared. She was a Forest girl again running to meet her brother, her own kind. She hugged him, wiped away a tear, instructed an inn servant to take his small pack of luggage up to his room, and suggested that they went to a coffee house to talk. They emerged from the inn yard and went off in the opposite direction from where her coach waited.

The coffee house was worn, solid and dark. The beams in the ceiling showed signs of woodworm. The windows panes were grey with dust, and the walls between the windows were of rough panelled oak. The place was busy, and Hannah guided Warren to the back of the establishment. Politicians, scroungers and gentlemen from the large houses on the river front were chatting, with time to spare, over their coffee. They gazed idly at Hannah and Warren as they passed. The local merchants and shopkeepers, who sat with serious faces talking business, ignored them.

Warren was intrigued by the smell of coffee, the hubbub and the personalities of these strange people, and eyed them cautiously as he was propelled by Hannah to the rear. Here they sat down in an empty compartment where the high wooden backs to the seats ensured privacy. The waiter, a burly, middle-aged man, came up.

Hannah ordered the coffee; then she looked at her brother. She noticed how gauche he was, how uncomfortably he sat. He had his best suit on, and wore a collar and cravat that sat stiffly round his neck. But his awkwardness warmed him to her.

"Dear Warren," she said, and smiled. "How are you? How is mother?"

"Her be all right," he replied in his thick Forest accent. She asked about other relatives and friends, and he replied equally briefly.

"How are things generally in the Forest, then?" she asked.

His face showed more interest. "Bad," he said, simply. "No work, and no sign that there will ever be any." He was still concerned, she could see, with this one theme, this one obsession. "No food either. Young Mary Baldwin's baby died last week. They do reckon that him starved to death. Him were but three months old. Mary were so weak that her couldn't provide milk to keep him alive."

Hannah looked down. She had known Mary Baldwin.

"And it all be the fault of them foreigners taking over our pits so we've got no work or money. They comes to the Forest with no seats to their trousers, some

'... The Tun Inn in Fleet Street where the coaches from Gloucester stopped'

of them. And then, I don't know how, in a few months you see them riding around in their carriages telling Foresters what to do." Warren drew his cup of coffee nearer.

"Hannah, these people be hard masters. They would rather see a man killed in the pit than a horse, because they would have to buy a new horse." He drank some coffee to hide his emotion. "Hannah, I gets real angry when I sees what they be doing to our people. And the government don't help with them enclosing the land in the Forest so that they can grow more trees. And they don't take no notice when we gets pushed off the land and can't let our animals feed there." His voice cracked.

Hannah placed her hand over his. She was embarrassed.

"What can I say?" she said. There was a pause. "But you know, Warren, there has always been poverty and hunger in the Forest."

"Yes, but it has never been so bad as 'tis now. It be much worse since thee got out."

Hannah withdrew her hand. He was back on his old line, criticising her as he always used to. The tender feeling she had experienced on their meeting again after so many years had drained away. She held her hands together under the table.

"Yes, I got out as you put it. I seized my chance. It was the best thing I ever did in my life." She spoke defiantly.

"Aye. That were the difference between us," continued Warren. "Thee got out, thee looked after thysen. Thee didn't think about other people."

"What could I do for other people?" she snapped. 'I send mam some money every week. I can't send everyone in the Forest money. What do you think I could have done, anyway?"

Warren, pale now, looked away from her, the agony that had risen up in him was no better for his outburst.

"Warren, let us not go over all that ground again. I want to enjoy seeing you again. Tell me why you have come up to London."

Warren's annoyance subsided. She could see that he was formulating his thoughts to reply. Then he spoke with determination, but a determination, she decided, that was touched with fear.

"I be meeting some people." He paused. "About the Forest."

"I shouldn't think that there are many people in London who have ever heard of the Forest of Dean."

"Well, you be wrong. There be men up here interested in what goes on down in Dean. I've written to them, and they've written to me."

Hannah drank some coffee. "Who are these people?"

"They be interested in poor people, people who work in coal mines and ironworks and factories all over England. One of them be a lawyer who knows a lot about the Forest. He be going to take me to parliament and I be going to present a petition against this new Forest Bill."

Hannah was silent. She knew that William had presented a Bill about the Forest to the House of Commons only three weeks ago.

"I've read in the paper what Lord Lowther did say in Parliament about what be wrong with the Forest. But he do have it all wrong. He don't know what it be really like there. I'd dearly love to tell him. Hannah, I've come to ask thee a favour. Would thee ask Lord Lowther if I could see him, talk to him for a few minutes, like?"

Hannah was immediately on her guard. "I don't know whether he would see you. I don't think I can ask him." She paused. "My position is not easy, you know."

"It be most important. I be the secretary of the Free Miners' Association in the Forest. If you tell him that, he might see me." He paused. "Hannah, please do me this favour."

Hannah thought for a minute. Warren seemed so intent, so determined, yet so ingenuous, so vulnerable. Then she leaned forward, and put her hand over his and smiled.

"Yes, Warren, I'll ask him. I'll ask him tonight, and I will send you a message tomorrow."

Warren thanked her. He relaxed, and sat back and took a sip of his coffee. They sat silent for a minute. Then Hannah looked at her watch. "I must go," she said. "But we'll meet again before you go back. I've booked your room for three nights and the bill is paid. Have all the meals you want there. The landlord will send the bill on to me. Stay longer if you want to." She rose. "And I will ask Lord Lowther. But I must go now."

That evening she told William that her brother was in town.

"Didn't know you had a brother. What's he up in town for?"

"He's on business. He would like to see you for a few minutes if you would receive him. I should be grateful if you did."

"What about?" Williams sensed that the request for a favour of some sort was in the offing. But a man in his position was frequently asked for favours.

"About the Forest and the Foresters."

"Well, I don't know what I can do for him, my dear, but since you ask, I'll see him."

The next afternoon Hannah conducted Warren to William's study and introduced them. She did not know whether to stay or go. She decided to go, and waited in the sitting room on the other side of the hall, with the door open so that she would know when the interview was over. She picked up her embroidery.

The men talked for about twenty minutes. When she heard the study door open, she put down the embroidery and hurried into the hall. They seemed to be in a good mood, and Hannah felt relieved. They continued chatting as she joined them, but it was clear that William considered the interview to be over. He made an excuse and returned to his study.

Hannah said briefly, "Let's go upstairs." Her satin dress swished softly, but her blue shoes were silent as she trod delicately over the red hall carpet and up the staircase. Warren followed clumsily in his big rough boots. In the annexe they went into Hannah's sitting room. She invited him to sit down, and he did so hesitantly. His rough, homespun suit, clean and brushed though it was, contrasted deeply with the patterned silk of the chair he sat on.

Hannah ordered tea. Charlotte wandered in and sat quietly at her mother's side. Hannah introduced her, but Warren showed little interest. She was, however, interested in him, and looked at him with unblinking eyes, trying to assess what sort of a man this uncle was.

Hannah asked how the interview had gone.

"Well enough, I suppose," Warren said. He sat awkwardly, balancing a cup of tea and a plate of wafer-thin white bread and butter on his lap. "I told him about the poverty that there be in the Forest these days and the causes of it, see, and asked him if he could do anything, him being an important person and Chief Commissioner of Woods, like. He did listen, I will say that, and he seemed sympathetic. He asked some questions, and we talked for quite a time. Then he said he would think about what I did tell him."

As he spoke, Hannah's heart pained her. She looked at his honest eyes. He was such an innocent in the wide world, a leader in the Forest, perhaps, but no match for the educated, smooth upper-class politician that was William. She did not think that Warren had achieved much.

"Well, he did say that he had sympathy for the Foresters, and that he would think about what you told him," was all she said. Then she added, "If anyone can do anything, Warren, he can."

For the first time since he had greeted her on descending from the coach at the Tun Inn, Warren now showed some interest in Hannah and her circumstances. He gave a faint smile, and warmth tinged his face as he leaned towards her.

"He be a nice fellow, your man," he said. That was all. But he meant it. He placed his cup and saucer carefully on a side table.

"I'd better be going now, I suppose," he said. "And I do thank thee for arranging for me to see him, though what good 'twill do, I don't know."

Loath to let him go, she put out her hand as he rose.

"Before you go, Warren, tell me more about these people you are seeing up here in London."

Warren sat down again. "Them as is interested in all working folk everywhere like. People who be willing to help us get rid o' the foreigners."

"You'll never get rid of the foreigners, Warren," said Hannah impatiently. "I don't know who these people are, but I wouldn't trust them if I were you."

"I know what I be doing."

"Maybe you think you do. But you are meddling with danger. Why don't you leave it all alone, and go back to the Forest? Content yourself with doing a good day's work, and enjoy what little leisure you have. Go out drinking with the other men. Find yourself a lass. Leave all this political stuff alone. For that's what it is, politics, and it can be dangerous. Warren, leave it alone."

Warren looked at her. "I can't," he said simply. "You knows that." He thought for a few seconds then, realising that he would get no encouragement from his sister, got up, thanked her again for her help and departed. That was the last time she saw him.

A month later the government in which William was a junior minister fell. It could resist no longer the demand for parliamentary reform. The Whigs took power and William had reluctantly to hand over his post at the Office of Woods to another. Hannah was not concerned for herself - the arguments between Whigs and Tories did not seem to her to relate to life as she knew it, but she was concerned because of the effect the dismissal of his party from power had on William.

"But the Tories will get back," she sympathised. "You've told me so often that they are the natural party of government in this country."

"Yes, but when? I was just on the point of getting a cabinet position. The prime minister had as good as promised me." He shrugged his shoulders, half irritably, half resignedly. "Still, I suppose that there is still a chance of our forming a government if the Whigs make a hash of reform. And then I will be all right if Wellington is asked to form another administration. Provided nothing else happens to damn my chances."

"What else can happen?" asked Hannah.

But the months went on, the Whigs did not make a hash of reform, and Wellington was not invited to form a government. William's initial annoyance and disappointment were replaced by frustration. Hannah encouraged him to go out and about more often with his friends, to have dinner parties more frequently at home and to pay more visits to his stud farm at Epsom. She encouraged him to enter his 3-year-old colt - named at her suggestion 'Forest Green'- for the 1831 Derby stakes and to spend more time watching its training. With satisfaction Hannah watched him become calmer and more patient. She had more of his company now and, forgetting her worries about the future, she entered on a phase in her life that gave her great happiness. It lasted several months.

And then it happened. One morning Hannah stayed in bed rather late. William was up promptly, as usual, but Hannah had a breakfast tray sent in. She ate a little, drank some coffee and then got up. She placed the tray on the table at the foot of the bed, and went over to the window. Outside the sun was shining and a slight wind ruffled the trees and caused a shifting pattern of light and shade on the ground. Across the road by the edge of the park she could see two servant girls talking to some soldiers. They held their bonnets by the ribbons and were swinging them as they smiled up at the guardsmen. The soldiers said something that amused them, and they all laughed. The men moved a fraction nearer to the girls.

It's the same everywhere, thought Hannah. flirting, amusing oneself, when one has the opportunity. She thought of the girls from the Forest. It was the same there. She left the girls to their soldiers.

Back in her room she felt lazy, and was in no mood to ring for her maid and start dressing, although she was going with William to Epsom to the Derby that afternoon. She sat down at her dressing table, and looked in the mirror. Nowadays she would often sit like this in the mornings, searching her face for lines that would make her less atractive to William. But not today. She stretched her arms upwards and admired the curve of her breasts through her nightdress. She smiled and shook her head so that her hair swirled round. She felt pleased with herself and with life.

Suddenly the door burst open. William stormed in. He kicked the table at the foot of her bed as he advanced towards her, and knocked the coffee pot onto the floor.

"Oh, look out, William," she said, "the coffee will stain the carpet. It's a new one."

"Damn the carpet."

He had in his hand several copies of the day's newspapers. He waved them at her.

"Your wretched brother has been stirring up trouble in the Forest."

Hannah rose to her feet.

"There have been some riots there, and according to *The Times* he is the leader."

Hannah suddenly felt very vulnerable, and pulled her dressing gown round her.

"The Foresters are breaking down all the enclosure walls. I'm not so much worried about that as I'm no longer the Chief Commissioner of Woods. But listen to this: 'There are persons of wealth, rank and parliamentary influence backing Warren James. These backers must be discovered'."

He handed the newspaper to her and she searched, unseeing, for the words he had read out.

"And listen to this from *The Globe:* 'Warren James is the agent of some one or more noblemen in town who are determined to see the Foresters righted. A sister of Warren James, it is said, lives with a nobleman, and James has been to town to have interviews on this business'."

Hannah stood silent, her hand to her throat.

"*The Globe* thinks it would not be prudent to mention names, but *The Times* is not so reticent," he continued. He seized *The Times* from her again, and read: "'The miners say that Lord Lowther is well disposed to the Foresters'.""

"Oh, God," said Hannah.

"See where your urging me to talk with your brother has placed me."

"I am sure Warren would not have put round these stories," said Hannah, recovering.

"I did not like him when I met him, and it was against my initial feelings that I ever saw him," he continued. His blood surged up as he seized her by the shoulders and stared hard and cold into her face.

"This is what happens when you get mixed up with people from the labouring classes."

He released her and stood back, aghast at what he had said. But he had thought it and it was out.

"William, that's not worthy of you. You knew all about my background when you took me up."

The door opened, and they both looked round. Hannah's maid entered cautiously. She handed William a letter. "This has just arrived, sir. The messenger says it is very urgent."

The letter was headed Apsley House, and ran: 'My dear Lowther, I should esteem it a great favour if you would come round at eleven. Wellington.' William showed it to Hannah.

"What does this mean?" she said.

"It means that Wellington wants to know all about it. At a time when the party are hoping to get back to power, this little scandal won't help. It certainly won't help me to that seat in the cabinet."

He took out his watch. "It's nearly eleven. I must go."

Hannah sat down, white-faced and exhausted. She had never seen William in such a fury. She went over what he had said in his onslaught, again and again. Then she slowly realised that in his reaction to the news that he so unexpectedly read in the papers he had been concerned only about himself. *He* had been slighted. *He* had been humiliated. *He* had had his chances of becoming a cabinet minister frustrated. Nothing else had entered his mind. He had not thought for a second how *she* might respond to her brother's actions and the situation he had placed himself in.

But that was not all. The effect of the revelations in the papers on her relationship with him now bore down on her. All London would now know of his mistress's connection with the leader of the riots. They would conclude that this was all her work. This was how she had served him. This was all her meddling. Hannah could hear them.

'The sister of a common little rioter from the Forest of Dean.'

'She must have been telling her brother all about Lord Lowther's business while he was Chief Commissioner.'

'Shows the effect a woman like that can have on a public man.'

Later in the morning she was standing by the window in the sitting room, thinking, thinking, thinking. She decided to go and see Mrs Dawson Damer, and then remembered that she was away in the country for a month. She burst into tears.

At that moment Mrs Beale, the housekeeper, came into the room.

"Madam, what's the matter?" she said.

Hannah ran over to her - she would have run over to anyone who had entered at that moment - and stood helplessly before her, unable to decide what to do, unable to control her tears. Mrs Beale took her hands, and Hannah was grateful for the human contact.

"Madam, what's the matter?" she repeated.

Hannah allowed Mrs Beale to put her arms round her shoulders. But there was no comfort in the cold black crispness of Mrs Beale's starched dress, and she drew back. She saw that the faint smile that always played round Mrs Beale's cheekbones had broadened a little.

She knew. All the servants knew. And they were glad, she was certain. Mrs Beale turned away, but the way she did so showed Hannah that she knew that soon she would once again be the only influential woman in the establishment.

William did not return to Carlton House Terrace until late afternoon. After the encounter with Mrs Beale, Hannah had stayed in her own private sitting room. William came in. She could see that he was still enraged, and had no sympathy for her despite her defencelessness. As she looked up at him, she knew that he wanted to hurt her, although she doubted if he would do her physical violence.

He went over the events again and again. Hannah offered some defence, but only half-heartedly. She knew she could not stand up against him. Finally she said, "I think I had better leave you."

"Yes," he responded, as he looked out of the window. "Perhaps that would be best."

Hannah drew back. Her offer had been unthinking, but it had been made, and she could not retract it.

"I will go tomorrow. When the Duke of Wellington knows that I have gone, he may be better disposed towards you."

"Yes, yes."

"I will take Charlotte with me."

His thoughts were still on other things. His political future means more to him than his domestic happiness, thought Hannah. She left the room, went into her bedroom and called her maid. She gave instructions to pack some things for herself and Charlotte.

Her maid said, "Are we going for long?"

"Charlotte and I are going: You are not. Pack enough for us that we can conveniently take on a stage coach, no more. Mrs Beale will tell you what your future duties will be."

A puzzled maid began to pack.

Hannah sat down at her dressing table. William's reply when she had offered to leave had stricken her to her heart. Did he really mean it? Perhaps he would ask her to stay when he had had a few hours to think. But if he did not, she would go. She would not plead with him.

Fortunately, she remembered, she had money stored away, money saved from the generous allowance he had made her. She was pleased now that she had been so prudent.

However, there were the jewels. She went to the dressing table and lifted out her jewel box. She took them out one by one, until there remained but one at the bottom of the box, a simple gold necklace, the one William had bought for her in Oxford on their first day together. She put it aside, replaced the other jewels in the box and went downstairs with it.

She found William in his study. "You had better have these back," she said, putting the box on his desk. "They are yours." She tried to restrain her bitterness but found herself saying, "You may need them again."

Drawn from his thoughts, William looked up at her coldly. "I gave them to you because I wanted you to have them. But I fear that it is all over now. It must be all over. Whatever one thinks in the early days, such liaisons have to end. And now ours has. Keep the jewels. They are yours."

Hannah waited to see if he would say more. She looked at him, her eyes anxious that he would do so. When he did not, she thanked him quietly for being so generous, and began to leave the room. There was no more to say.

But, as she was leaving, he said, "Get in touch with my lawyers. I will arrange for them to make a settlement."

The next morning Hannah ordered her carriage for the last time, told Charlotte that they were going on holiday in the Forest of Dean, and drove with her to a bank in Threadneedle Street. Here she deposited the jewels, saying she would give instructions about them later. Then she went to Fleet Street, booked seats on the next coach to Gloucester, and sent the carriage back to Carlton House Terrace. They had an hour to wait before the coach left, and they spent it in the coffee house which Hannah had visited with Warren.

On the first stage of the journey to the Forest Hannah went over the events of the last 24 hours again. It was, indeed, only a day since William had burst into her bedroom and the bomb had exploded. She had known from the beginning that a mistress could not expect the same treatment as a wife, and realised now that she had always known in her heart that she would not live at Carlton House Terrace for ever. Then she remembered that Mrs Dawson Damer had told her about Kitty Lane who had retained the affections of old Lord Exeter for forty years until she died. But that was an exception. The bond between her and

William had clearly not been as strong; it had not been able to resist the revelations of yesterday's newspapers.

She wondered whether William would ask her to come back when the present turmoil had died down. He had accepted her suggestion that she should leave with the same lack of thought that she had shown when she offered it. Had he not been so frustrated at being thwarted in his political advancement, he might have thought matters through more clearly. Or was he already tiring of her and using the situation as an excuse to separate?

If he did not invite her to come back, would he remember her with at least some affection? When King George had died the previous year Mrs Dawson Damer had told her that he had been buried with a diamond locket round his neck containing a miniature portrait of Mrs Fitzherbert. From what Hannah had heard from people who knew him, George IV had been an insensitive, bad-tempered pig; but he had clearly been capable of keeping his love for Mrs Fitzherbert during all the 25 years that he had been cut off from her. In her anguish Hannah was sure that William would not remember her with such fidelity in 25 years time.

Hannah had bought a copy of *The Times* as she and Charlotte had boarded the stage coach in London. She had forgotten about it, but now took it from her bag and began to search for the latest news of the Forest riots. Before she found it, however, her eye caught a more prominent headline about the Derby. *Forest Green* had won! Hannah smiled cynically. What did winning a horse race matter now? Yet at the same time, her heart went out to him. Winning the Derby had meant so much to him; and he hadn't been there to see his horse win. Well, he hadn't, and that was that.

She continued her search for information about the riots, and learnt that the military had been called to the Forest and had made short work of the disturbances. The riots were over, the Foresters had fled to avoid capture, and were hiding in barns, under beds, anywhere where they might be safe. Warren, it seemed, had hidden in the pit where he worked, the Work or Hang pit, an ironically named place, Hannah thought. Someone knowing his whereabouts, one of his colleagues the paper suggested, had betrayed him to the authorities. No-one had dared to descend into the darkness of the pit knowing that he was at the bottom waiting for them, so the soldiers had enticed him up by pretending that one of his family wished to speak with him. On emerging from the pit shaft a dozen soldiers had surrounded him and taken him to Coleford for interrogation. He was now in Gloucester gaol awaiting trial on a charge of felony, for which the penalty, she read, was death by hanging without the benefit of clergy. Tears prevented Hannah from reading more, but she realised how impossible his situation was. The government would make him the scapegoat for the riots, and he would almost certainly be found guilty and executed.

"Oh, Warren, Warren," she cried within herself. "Why did you do it?"

And as she asked the question she knew the answer. Warren had no more been able to resist doing what he could for his fellow Foresters than she had been able to resist Lord Lowther's enticement to leave the Forest and go and live with him. Both had done what their natures had dictated. And, ultimately, both, in their own way, had failed.

The coach lumbered into Coleford and pulled up at the Angel Inn in the Market Place. The four young men jumped down from the top of the coach and disappeared inside the inn demanding savaloys and porter.

"We are here," said the fat gentleman. "We are at Coleford." He looked at Hannah, expecting some response. But she sat, oblivious to him. After a few seconds he raised his eyebrows, got to his feet, opened the coach door and, breathing heavily, began to climb down the steps. Soon he was busy supervising the unloading of his luggage.

"Mamma, we are here," said Charlotte.

Hannah looked at her and smiled. "Yes, dear, we are here." They collected their things and got out of the coach.

The warm chatter of Coleford Market Place surged around her. She heard the friendly accents of the people as, in their gentle way, they went about their business. Enoch was standing waiting for them. He smiled and opened his arms wide. She ran to him.

The past was over. Hannah was back in the Forest.

THE MINERS' FUND

Jimmy paused at the end of the lane. He had to make a decision, the same decision that confronted him every day on his way home from school. Should he go to the village shop first and look in its window?

It was nearly tea-time and he was hungry. Even so, he decided to go to the shop.

Jimmy was 8 years old. He had one of those faces from which you could deduce what he would look like when he was 50. He had never fully recovered from scarlet fever earlier in the year, and his face under his thin straight hair was pale with that tinge of grey that characterises so many undernourished children. His eyes were dark and looked steadily and suspiciously through eyelids that never seemed to be fully opened. His short trousers were threadbare, his socks drooped around his ankles, and his plimsoll laces trailed the ground.

The shop had once been a private house and its window had been the sitting-room window. It now displayed a large number of goods that could be bought within, but there was no order in the display. The shopkeeper had squeezed in extra goods whenever he deemed they needed to go on show, and in so doing had submerged other items already there. Knitting wool and bootlaces nudged a packet of biscuits; a card advertising chocolate nestled among household brushes; a miniature china tea-set, a model car and a doll sat precariously on a big box of 'Sunny Jim' corn flakes. Almost a year ago they had been placed on show as part of a Christmas display. The tinsel had been removed but the toys, their boxes faded by the summer sun, remained.

The whole window showed neglect, and the reason was simple. The shopkeeper had lost heart. No-one would buy the toys; few people bought chocolates; in spite of Sunny Jim's bright appearance and energetic stance, no-one was interested in his corn flakes. After four months of the lock-out ordinary folk had no money for luxuries - they had little money for essentials. The shopkeeper was on the verge of bankruptcy.

But Jimmy was not looking at the chocolate advertisement or at Sunny Jim. He was looking at the toy car, made of tin and constructed, so the note on the box said, exactly like the original. He brushed some hair from his forehead and blinked as he continued to stare at the car. His face showed no emotion as his eyes went over its outline. He examined the little man in the driving seat, even to the pin pricks of eyes that some factory girl had given him. He envied that little man.

Then he turned, buttoned his coat (for it was getting cold) and went up the lane to the back entrance of his house. He shut the garden gate carefully behind him. One had to be careful. If the sheep that roamed free in the Forest got in, they would eat all his father's vegetables. He went down the path, and crossed by means of a plank the ditch that ran along the back of the row of cottages. The slops from the cottages flowed along the ditch when it rained. When there was no rain, they lay stagnant and smelt. They smelt now.

Jimmy stepped over the threshold into the kitchen. He noticed immediately that the big oil lamp had disappeared. It had no doubt been sold, like the ornaments and the pictures on the wall and most of the furniture. Only a few chairs, a cupboard and a table remained. The plastered ceiling showed in places its rib-like laths; and the rough stone walls, unadorned, seemed over-big for the room. Its bareness struck Jimmy anew as he took his coat off. He glanced at the baby, a puny creature of 12 months, who was sitting crying on a cushion on the flagstone floor.

Jimmy's father and uncle were on each side of the fire. With legs out-stretched and hands clasped in front of them, they were not men who had worked hard and were now relaxing, but bored men who had too much time to spare.

"Hello Dad, Uncle Bill, Mam." They returned his greeting.

The first thing one noticed about Jimmy's father, Milton, was the slit of coal across the bridge of his nose, a reminder of the blow from another lad's shovel on his first day in the pit. He was about 30, square-jawed and cheerful, tall with a stoop, broad but thin. He was getting thinner as the months went on, and had recently made an extra hole in his belt so that his trousers would hold up.

Uncle Bill was smaller than his brother, and older. His hair was thinning and his skin was stretched over his cheek bones. His eyes were friendly, but dark and penetrating. When he looked at you, you felt constrained to look away.

"Tea ready, Mam?" Jimmy was hungry. He was always hungry. There was always a tight feeling in his belly. Hunger was part of his body, part of his life.

"A few minutes," said his Mother. "Why don't you look at your car book until it be ready?"

She was pale-faced, nondescript. His lank hair had been bobbed - not too efficiently - by a neighbour. Her parents had christened her Marie Louise - for they had high hopes for her - but she was always called Mary. Tiredness oozed from her every movement.

Jimmy squeezed past his father, searching for his car book.

"I hears that there be about 350 men who 'ave gorn back to work," Milton was saying. "A couple o' months ago it were only 50. That be bad."

Jimmy did not understand. Bad that men were going back to work?

"Them that goes back want to remember that there be another day after today. Them blacklegs will carry disgrace with them as long as they live, you mark my words," said Uncle Bill.

The remark meant nothing to Jimmy, and he continued to search in the cupboard for his car book. He found it under an oak box. The box had a handle protruding from one end and a slit for coins in the top.

"Hey, Mam, what be this?"

"That be mine," said Milton. "It be my miners' fund box."

"Looks to me like it come from the Methodist Chapel," said Mary. She was cutting slices of bread for tea.

"Yes, I borrowed it."

"What be it for, Dad?"

"It be going with me to Cheltenham on Sunday, with the choir. We be taking banners and placards about the lock-out, and the choir will sing - make a noise to attract attention, like - and I'll use the box to collect anything people gives us. And we'll give the money we collects to the miners' fund."

"Can I come, Dad?"

"No, son, sorry."

Jimmy turned his eyes slowly from his father with no sign of the disappointment he felt, and put his car book on the table. It had been made from brown paper by his father and sewn together in the middle by his mother. In it he had pasted pictures of cars, all sorts of cars from Ford T models to foreign racing cars with unpronounceable names. Mostly they were in black and white, but a few were in colour. He turned the pages slowly, taking in lovingly every outline. He saw them all on the road or on the race track, and heard every splutter and roar. Then he took an old tobacco tin from the cupboard and examined his cigarette cards. Players had recently started a new series of domestic cars. He sorted out his swaps. Unfortunately, men in the village didn't smoke Players. When they were in work it was Woodbines. Now, if they smoked at all, they rolled their own.

"I want the table now, Jimmy. Move your stuff, there's a good boy," said Mary.

Jimmy did not move.

"Come on, Jimmy." She was cross now. "It's tea time." She had had a tiring day. Now strike pay had been cut, there was only parish relief, and most of the morning she had spent queueing at the Chapel, where the council men had set up their office. Then she had gone to the shop to turn her food notes into food. There had been a queue there, too. All the women were asking for more credit to eke out the food notes, but the shopkeeper was refusing to give any more food on tick.

Bill got up.

"Stop for a cup of tea, Bill?" said Milton.

"No. No, thanks. I be off." He found his cap from the collection of caps and coats behind the door, and left.

"I saw him looking at the bread," said Milton.

"He knows we 'aven't got no more than him," said Mary.

"Reckon he's got less."

Mary put a plate with three thick slices of bread spread thinly with margarine on the table, and poured out three cups of strong tea. She picked up the baby, sat him on a chair and gave him a crust and a mite of milk. Jimmy drew his chair up to the table and began to eat his slice of bread.

"Aye," said Milton. "Bill have got even less than we. I remember the day he got up at thic meeting during the '21 strike," he reminisced. "The employers were all up on the platform, their faces fat and lardy - old Bishop was there with all the others - and they was trying to tell us that it was in our interests to take a cut in wages and go back to work."

"Come and sit down and have your tea," said Mary.

"And Bill got up and started speaking. He were only a thin little man even then, but he seemed big, like, as he got up and spoke. And he started talking about us miners and how we had to live. Quiet at first and then louder. He told them straight what it was like to be a miner, and they up there on the platform 'ad to listen to 'im. I can't rightly remember now just what he did say, but I do remember seeing them look away from 'im, the shifty lot. They did look sideways and down. I saw Bishop's face drop and 'e didn't know where to look but at his fat belly. But they got their own back, mind. They blacklisted 'im all through the Forest after that, and he's never 'ad a proper job since."

Jimmy had stopped eating and was gazing at his father.

There was silence for a few seconds. Then Mary said, "And much good did that strike do you, or any of us. You had to give in in the end, just as you'll have to give in at the end of this one."

Jimmy finished eating his bread and margarine, and looked round. But he knew there was no point in asking for more. He was about to finish drinking his tea and get down when his mother produced a paper bag. From it she took half a ginger-nut biscuit and gave it to him.

He looked at it suspiciously.

"A bit of a treat for you," she said. "Now chew it, mind. I got a few ounces cheap at the stores," she said to Milton. "They was cheap because they was all broken, like."

Jimmy, finding the biscuit hard to break with his teeth, dipped it into his tea.

"Don't do that," said Mary. "It'll get all soft and you'll waste it. Chew it hard and it'll do you good."

The next day was Saturday, and Mary took Jimmy and the baby along to the soup kitchen that had been set up on the village football pitch. The soup kitchen had been organised, with much publicity, by Mrs Eleanor Bishop, the wife of the local pit owner. Mrs Bishop didn't come every day it operated, but she was there today, to supervise. She had thoughtfully put on her oldest coat, and as she glanced down at it she was glad no-one would see her in it. She took a deep breath as she surveyed the growing queue and ordered her assistant to start ladling out the glutinous concoction she called nourishing soup.

Mary eyed Mrs Bishop as the queue shuffled nearer. She envied her beautiful, thick, long coat, trimmed with fur, mauve and smooth, just like Queen Mary's. Indeed Mrs Bishop was very like the queen, with that firm, structured bosom that seemed composed of one breast without a parting rather than the usual two.

The baby in Mary's arms began to cry, a mechanical, tired, hopeless cry. Mrs Bishop looked at Mary sharply.

"Why is that child crying?"

"Because he's not well ma'am. That's why."

The baby stopped crying and shot a look at Mrs Bishop under his petulant dark eyebrows. He turned his face to his mother and nuzzled into her thin flat breast. His mouth opened, seeking blindly.

"There be no more there, my love," she whispered, more to herself than to the baby. "It's all gone now." She hugged him tightly and looked at Mrs Bishop.

Mrs Bishop, embarrassed, looked away, but her agressiveness remained.

"What's your name, boy?" she said to Jimmy.

"Jimmy - ma'am."

"Have you said your prayers today, Jimmy?"

Jimmy smelt danger. He looked straight at her, at her hard, powdered face, with unblinking eyes. "Yes, ma'am."

"Are you sure?"

"Yes, ma'am."

Mrs Bishop signalled majestically that Mary should be served, and Mary took a jugful of Mrs Bishop's bounty back home.

After dinner Jimmy went round to the shop, and was about to press his nose once more against its window when something unusual happened - a car drew up. The driver got out and entered the shop, leaving a middle-aged woman in the passenger seat. Jimmy barely noticed the people, but he saw the car. His eyes widened as he took it in. It was a Humber - big and brown, its metal shining, its leather seats gleaming. The hood was folded down at the back and was neatly enclosed in a light brown canvas cover. Jimmy moved to the back and noticed that it had a YY registration number, just like the one on his cigarette card. Over the petrol tank was a platform to which an elegant suitcase was strapped.

He walked into the road, looking at every part, every accessory. He examined the big spare wheel, nestling with its dozens of wire spokes into the front mud-guard. At the front he saw the headlights protruding like dragon's eyes, and the radiator cap standing proud and important. Jimmy decided that it was pure silver. He moved back on to the pavement, and gazed at his reflection in the passenger's door. As he looked up, he saw that the woman was smiling down at him from her seat.

"Do you like the car, then?" she said. She was not a Forester.

"Oh, yes," he replied, his tone excited, though not a muscle of his face moved.

"Have a chocolate," she said, and offered him a bag. He looked inside it. The chocolates were all the same, so he took the nearest.

"Thanks." He put the chocolate in his mouth and looked at her.

The man came out of the shop with a packet of cigarettes.

"This young man is admiring our car," she said.

"You like it, do you?"

"It be a 1924 Humber, bain't it?"

"Yes, indeed. Do you know a lot about cars?"

"Yes. Well, a bit."

"Would you like to sit in the driver's seat?"

"Can I?" And he allowed the man to lift him in. Poor little devil, the man thought, he seems so slight and unprotected.

Jimmy could not reach the foot pedals, but he could hold the steering wheel and touch the brake and gear levers. The lady smiled at him, but he was more interested in the car's interior. He looked at the horn.

"Can I?"

"Yes, have a go;" and Jimmy grasped the large rubber bulb of the horn. With an effort he succeeded in producing several breathy, raucous honks.

After a few more minutes Jimmy reluctantly got out.

"It be a lovely car," he said. He looked up at the man. "It be just like the one in the shop window." He pointed, and took the man's hand. Surprised at the intimacy, the man allowed Jimmy to lead him to the shop window. He could not understand why he felt so moved by this friendly ragamuffin.

"Would you - would you like to have the car in the window?"

Jimmy paused before he replied. "Yes, but I 'aven't got no money."

The man saw the price scribbled on the side of the box.

"Here's ninepence. Go and buy it for yourself." He patted Jimmy on the head. Then he climbed into the car and they drove off.

Jimmy looked at the ninepence, a silver sixpence and a silver threepenny bit. He looked at the car in the window, and paused for a moment, his face impassive. Then he closed his fingers round the money and went home.

He pushed open the kitchen door. His father was sitting by the fire. Jimmy took his hand and put the ninepence into it.

"What's this for, then? Where did you get this?"

"It's for the miners' fund, Dad."

THE TEASHOP

She chose a table by the window. Then she could see the people in the street as they passed. Leisurely, they were, with no stress or strain, just going about their business with the occasional smile, looking into the small shops that edged the street, at peace with themselves.

The waitress came up. As she ordered a pot of tea and a scone, she was aware that the waitress was examining her clothes and her face. She knew that she was extremely well dressed and exquisitely made up for such a teashop or, indeed, for any teashop. Even so, she glanced down at her cashmere suit, and took out her make-up bag and examined her face in the mirror, just in case something had happened. Her suit and her face were fine, her face especially so. These days it looked its best in a subdued light.

A young couple came in, married she would guess by the way he entered first. There were two seats free at her table. The man hesitated, but the woman pushed him forward, and they sat down further on. She smiled. She was used, even at her age, for women to push their menfolk past her. Anyway, they did not look interesting and she wanted someone to talk to.

She had just spent an hour looking round the town she had once known so well. It had grown a lot since she had last been there. She had been concerned that they had knocked down that old building in the middle of the market place. She had loved it so much, and now there was a great void. They had probably done it to ease the traffic. The big buses could never get round comfortably, even in her day.

She didn't approve of all these changes, but it was good to be back. After two abortions, three husbands and four face lifts, she'd had enough. She needed a rest. She wanted to relax.

An elderly man entered the teashop. He was neatly dressed, but his raincoat was old-fashioned. Probably a pensioner with not much money, she thought. He hesitated at her table, but after looking at her decided to move on. However, there was no seat available, so he came back.

"Is this anyone's seat?" he asked timidly.

"No. Please sit down," she replied with a smile. She moved her handbag from the table and put it on the floor.

He sat down awkwardly, dismissed a thought with a slight sniff, and looked out of the window. He glanced at her sideways once or twice. She was not surprised. Men were always looking at her.

The waitress came up for his order.

"Can I have a cup of tea and a cake, please?" he said.

He was a mild little man, about her age. He reminded her of someone. But then she had known so many men.

His tea and cake arrived.

"Can you pass the sugar, please?"

"Of course," she replied with a smile. Too late she realised that the smile was over-generous. She did not want to scare him.

"Do you come from round here?" she asked.

"Er, yes. I live just outside the town. I come in every Friday to collect my pension at the post office, do a bit of shopping, like, and then come in here for a cup of tea. Ethel used to come with me. Until last year, that is."

There was a pause. The conversation was not very exciting, and had now dried up; but she liked him and she had nothing else to do but chat.

"They make a good cup of tea here," she said. One could always talk about the quality of the tea and the weather.

The idea had not occurred to him.

"Yes, I suppose they do," he responded.

"I came in because my feet were killing me. I'd parked my car and was having a good walk round. I used to live near here, you know. This teashop used to be a greengrocer's."

She had aroused his interest.

"Yes, it did, I remember. But that was a long time ago. Thirty years or more." He looked at her curiously. "Where did you live, then?"

"Oh, about half a mile from here along the Newland road. There were two cottages near the railway line. I expect they've knocked them down now."

"No, they haven't. They're still there. I live in one of them. Lived there all my life."

She put down her cup. "You aren't Len Phelps, are you?"

"Yes, that's me. If you lived next door, you must be Susie Lambert. But you can't be. Even without - even after all those years, I should be able to recognise you a bit, but I can't." He was unwinding at last.

"It's strange being called Susie Lambert. No-one has called me that for forty years."

"Why not, if it's your name?"

"Well, you see, I changed my name."

He nodded, but he didn't understand.

"So you still live in the same house, then. Who lives in our house?"

"An old couple. They've been there about two years. Come from London, I think. Nice people. But they altered things. They dug up the vegetable patch. It was your father's pride and joy. And they planted a lawn there. You can't eat a lawn."

Susie smiled. Then she remembered she must not flash that famous smile too often. It embarrassed him.

"When did we last meet, Len? May I call you Len?"

"I reckon I last saw you when I was about twelve, though I hadn't seen much of you for some time before that. You won a scholarship to the grammar school, didn't you?"

"Yes."

"I stayed at the elementary school until I was 14. Then you left the district, as I remember."

"Yes, that's right. We went to live in Monmouth."

He sipped his tea. "We used to have good fun, you and me when we were kids." His face showed that he was dredging his memory for childhood recollections of Susie. "We were good mates, you and me. Do you remember we used to play in that old cottage over the road that wasn't lived in after old Mrs Turley died? Falling to bits, it was."

"Yes, we used to swing on the beams with the other children. It's a wonder we didn't hurt ourselves."

"And how we used to hang on the backs of trains as they went up the hill, slow like?"

"And the guard got so cross when he saw us," she said.

Bonds forged half a century earlier were discovered.

"Aye, we had some good fun." He looked at her elegant hair and her delicately rouged cheeks. "You were a proper tomboy then. What happened after you left?" he said.

"I was at school in Monmouth until I was 17. Then I went to a dancing school."

"Yes, I remember you were always dancing about as a girl."

"And I became a professional dancer on the stage. Then I met my first husband. He was a producer. He was older than me. He found me a good part in a London show." She did not tell him that she had had to sleep with him to get it.

"He changed my name to Suzette Lamont. Did you ever hear of it?"

He did not reply.

"And from then on I starred in one west end show after the other."

"Oh, aye," he said, but he did not appear to take in what she was saying.

"Then I went to America."

"Is your husband with you today?"

"No, I divorced him. But I married again after a few years. My new husband was my leading man in *Tootsie Wootzie*. A handsome fellow, he was, charming on stage and off. Unfortunately, after six months' marriage he was always charming some other woman."

"He died," she said sadly. In fact, she had divorced him, too, and a third; but she didn't think she dared burden Len with too much detail.

"The Americans loved me. I did four musicals on Broadway, one after the other. One was a Cole Porter."

"Oh aye." She didn't believe he had ever heard of Cole Porter.

"But what about you Len? What have you done?"

"Well, I went down the pit when I left school, and worked there until it closed down in 1960."

"Weren't you in the army during the war?"

"No, I was in a reserved occupation. Digging coal were hard work, but I liked it. I never got used to working in a factory afterwards."

"In a factory?"

"After the pit closed down, I was lucky to get a job in a factory in Gloucester. It was shift work. There was three shifts a day, and we had to do all three over a period of six weeks."

"How did you get there? Did you have a car?"

"No. The firm laid on their own buses to collect us. Outside the *Angel* at six in the morning, it was, two in the afternnon and ten at night. They brought us back, of course."

"That reminds me of a musical I was once in, *Froth and Bother*. It was about a woman who was on shift work and her husband never knew which shift she was supposed to be on."

"We didn't have no women on our shifts."

"They made it into a film, though the film version wasn't so good as the stage. Did you see it? I was in it."

"We didn't ever go to the pictures. Ethel didn't like the pictures. Anyway we had the kids to look after of an evening. We was quite happy sitting at home, listening to the wireless. Later, of course, we had the telly."

"I was never on television, except on chat shows. It was too late for me."

He adjusted his hearing aid. "Yes. We used to go to bed early."

Susie recalled that one of her childhood dreams had been that she would marry Len.

"Len, I want to ask you something. Have you had a happy life?"

Len had never thought about it. Life was life. You just took it as it came. He supposed he had. He had married Ethel. They had got on well together. He was sorry she was gone, but there it was. Nowadays he went down to the pub at night, and the fellows were friendly.

"I suppose so," he replied. "I have two lovely children who are very good to me, and half a dozen grandchildren that are always crawling over me. I dig a bit in the garden, and I've got my old age pension. It's not much, but I don't go hungry."

She was silent for a moment. When he did not return her question, she said,

"Well, I've had an exciting life. It's been hectic, but lovely. No regrets. But now it's all over. I've retired from the stage. And I can't really say that I am sorry."

"What are you doing in Coleford, then? Visiting?"

"No. I don't know anyone here - except you. I've come to look for a house to retire into. All the years I've been away I've thought, 'One day I'll go back to the Forest of Dean and buy a lovely cottage, roses round the door, and all that. I'll have wonderful neighbours to talk to, and I'll buy a little dog and take it for walks in the Forest. I'll not have any servants - they are only a nuisance - I'll just have a woman to come in every day and a man to do the garden'."

She poured herself another cup of tea.

"And now the time has come. I've got enough money to live comfortably. And I've got my alimony. I'm living in London at the moment, but it's only temporary. I was at an estate agent's half an hour ago and he gave me details of a lovely cottage not far from here, four bedrooms and half an acre of ground. And I'm on my way to see it now."

She showed him the estate agent's leaflet. He did not read the words, but looked at the picture.

"I know that place. It's up at the crossroads. I went inside it once. It's a big house," he said. "But I expect your husband will help fill it. I suppose your children are grown up."

"I've no husband and no children."

"Oh." He thought about it. Then he looked at his watch. "Well, I must go and catch my bus. I hope you like the house."

He got up, went to the cash desk and paid his bill. Then he left the tearoom without a glance back.

He hadn't said he would see her again. She sat looking out of the window. It was getting dark and beginning to rain. Women were hurrying home to get tea for their men. She felt tired and old, and alone. The face that a few minutes earlier had been so pink and animated was now an old face, painted and powdered.

If she was going to inspect the cottage she must go soon. But she thought she wouldn't go today. In fact she didn't want to go at all. She did not want to retire to the Forest. She would go back to her flat in Chelsea.

She paid the bill, put a tip under the plate, and left the teashop.

PIRATE TREASURE

Some years ago Alec, a friend of mine who lived at Tidenham, told me a curious story about pirates burying treasure in the Forest of Dean. He had forgotten who had told him this, and did not remember where the treasure was supposed to be hidden. I laughed and forgot all about it. But a few years later I made a discovery that reminded me of his story.

I was doing some research into the life of a man named Morse for a book I was writing about the Forest village of Parkend. Morse had lived there at the beginning of the 19th century, and I went to the Gloucestershire Record Office to see if they had any documents about him. There was nothing in their index, but a member of the staff suggested that I should look in a box marked "M", which had some documents in it that had not yet been examined and indexed. I thought this a good idea, and in ten minutes an attendant placed a large box on the table before me.

The box was old, and its leather cover was worn. I guessed that it had begun life in a solicitor's office holding deeds and wills. A mouldy smell arose as soon as I opened it. Before me were dozens of old documents, all dirty and dusty, and of various shapes and sizes. Some were tied with red tape, some with white tape and some with string. They had been folded for so long that it was difficult to keep them open while I examined them. They were mostly from the 19th century - letters, memoranda, drafts and accounts - though some were older. The only thing they had in common was that they were all signed with a name beginning with "M".

I examined each one carefully, and when I had finished placed them in a pile on the desk. Not one related to "my" Morse, or any other Morse for that matter. Disappointed, I started to return the documents to the box. As I did so I saw on the back of one of them an address, "Port Royall, Jamaica". This intrigued me, and I unfolded the letter. It read as follows:

Montego Bay, Jamaica.
23rd day of January, 1688

To Master Robert Burney,
Thames Street, Port Royall, Jamaica.

My dear Robert,

The merrie Night of drinking you and I did have in December last in that Inne at Port Royall with much good Discourse about our Combats against the perfidious Spaniards in times past is no doubt still alive in your Memory as it is in mine. As I did say on that occasion I am very sensible of the great Service you did me at Portobello all those Years since, when you did leap down on some Dogg of a Spaniard about to plunge his Knife into my Back, the first I remember of the Encounter being when his Head came flying through the Air severed by you from his loathsome Body by the Stroke of your Cutlass. It is this fearless Act for which I shall be forever beholden to you that is the chief Business of this Epistle.

I am become old and fat, being much given to drinking and sitting up late, which so my Physician informs me is the Cause of the Dropsie with which I am afflicted. In truth I perceive that God may not grant me many more months on this Earth. When I depart my Life I shall go as a respected Inhabitant of this Island and a Man of Substance with my several Plantations and a large Personal estate. Yet in addition to all my Wealth here, I have in England an even greater Store, more than anyone can conceive. Because of my Condition I have neither physical Ability nor Desire to go to England to get it, but I conceive that after all the Blood and connivance necessitated by its Obtainance it must not be left hidden for all Eternity where it at present lieth.

Because of my Beholdenness to you I give you this Wealth. As you no doubt have guessed, it is Spanish Treasure. I took it at the Sack of that famous and antyent Citty of Panama, the greatest Mart for Silver and Gold in the whole World, which you remember was ravaged so thoroughly and severely by my great Fleet of Privateers 17 years past. While John Morris who was the Captain of the *Dolphin* and I were in Company turning over the Storeroom of the Palace of the President of Panama we came upon a great Chest filled with the most exquisite Jewells, Diamonds, Emeralds, Rubys of the choicest Kind and Quantities of Gold, a Ransom fitt for a King. I truly believe that this Horde was prepar'd ready to be transported to the Galleon that departed in haste on the verry Day we arriv'd on the Outskirts of Panama. Captain Morris and I did conclude that the Treasure was too precious a Haul to contribute to the common Pool to be distributed among the men and (illegible) in secret to a friend of mine from my old Days in England and leave it hidden there until the Rage and Recriminations over Panama had subsided. My friend was named John Witt who was Keeper of the Kinge's Coleworks in the Forrest of Deane in Glostershire where I visited him many Times in earlier Days. He and Captain Morris did burry the Treasure near his House as is shown on the accompanying map. They (illegible) Treasure should be rested in the very place that hath produced Treasure of another kind for the Forrest.

Almost immediately after the Captain did return to Jamaica I was apprehended and enforcedly removed to England on matters arrising from the sack of Panama. However, after I was freed and before I returned to Jamaica I was able to visit my friend in the Forrest of Deane and confirmed that the Treasure was indeed safe but I deemed it wise considering the Circumstances of my enforced Visit to England to leave it where it was hid.

Last Month I heard that the Captain had dyed of a fever. Furthermore I did last Weeke have Newes come to me that my Friend in England had dyed also. So it was borne in on me (illegible) where the Treasure is hid but me and I am unable to reach it.

Goe and gett it, my dear Robert. Gett it and enjoy it in Appreciation of your great Act of saving my Life.

With my good Wishes for your Successe and Enjoyment thereof.

HENRY MORGAN

I read it twice. Feeling that I had discovered a great secret that no one else must know about, I looked round to see if anyone was watching me. Casually I went to the duplicating machine and made a copy to take away and study. I replaced the original in the box and returned it to the counter.

"Any luck?" said the member of staff who had recommended that I should look in it.

"Er, no," I replied. Then, feeling that I must make my reply a little more honest, I added, "Nothing about anyone called Morse." With that I left the Record Office.

In a nearby café over a cup of tea I examined my copy of Morgan's letter again. Was it a hoax? Who was this man Morgan who lived in Jamaica? It seemed that he was a pirate of some sort. But a pirate connected with the Forest of Dean? Treasure in the Forest? I could not believe it. It must be a joke. Perhaps a very old joke, perhaps a seventeenth or eighteenth century joke. But a joke.

Nevertheless, I thought, it could be true. It would certainly be more interesting to follow it up than to continue research into the affairs of Mr Morse of Parkend.

The next day I visited my local library in the lunch hour, and took out every book they had on pirates and privateers in the Caribbean. I spent the next few evenings reading them and making notes. So this was Henry Morgan's world! A world that I had previously known nothing about, a world teeming with excitement, brutality, greed, double-dealing, fighting and murder.

When I had read all the books I had borrowed I phoned Alec and said that I had something interesting to tell him and he must come over. He came the following evening. My wife had gone to bed with a cold and a hot water bottle before he arrived, so we had the house to ourselves. It had been a dull unpleasant day with a sad-looking sky, and it was becoming increasingly cold. Snow began to fall as Alec arrived. I had a big log fire burning in the sitting room and he stretched out his hands thankfully towards it as he sat down. A hot cup of tea thawed him out. I looked at him as he began to sip it. He was only 35, a few years younger than myself, but was, I thought, beginning to look old. Or was it the cold journey that made him grey and drawn? He looked up and his cheerful grin - I could never decide whether he consciously turned it on or whether it was natural - transformed his face. The wrinkles at the sides of his eyes became less sad as he sipped his tea gratefully.

I turned the centre lights out so that we were lit only by one side lamp and the fire. He leaned back in his armchair, relaxed and crossed his long legs.

"Well, what's this all about, then?" he said.

I realised that the story I was proposing to tell him was fantastic. Here we were in a warm, comfortable room with calm and friendship surrounding us and I was about to talk about - pirate treasure! I wondered what his reaction would be.

"You remember you told me ages ago that there was pirate gold hidden in the Forest?" I began.

He looked up. "Yes, vaguely," he said.

"Well, I think you were right."

He smiled. "You didn't believe me at the time."

"You couldn't remember where you got the story from."

"I have an idea I read it when I was researching for a novel about ten years ago. But go on."

I told him the story of my discovery at the Record Office, of my disbelief at first, and how I had gradually come to the conclusion that Henry Morgan's letter was authentic. I handed him my copy of it. He read it carefully, and thought for a moment.

"This is only a photocopy, of course," he said. "And look at these gaps in the text. It looks as if rats have gnawed at the original."

I waited. Then he said, "How do you know that this all stands up? Anyone

'Henry Morgan... spent ten years raiding Spanish merchant ships and pillaging Spanish towns and villages on the Main'

could have written this."

"To start with I think the letter is genuine. The paper is 17th century, I'm sure. It's made from rag, not your modern stuff that disintegrates after thirty years. And the contents ring true."

"I expect you have been doing some research on it." He looked up at me and grinned.

"Of course," I grinned back. "The first thing I must tell you is that Henry Morgan was a real person. There's no doubt about that. Here's a picture of him."

I handed Alec a faded reproduction of a portrait of Morgan that I had unearthed. Here was no romantic, carefree pirate, but a respectable, middle-aged citizen, dressed in glorious satin with a silk bow round his neck. A trim moustache in the fashion of the upper classes proclaimed respectability. But an inner power shone through, and full lips and steady, bulging eyes revealed a cruelty that had long before manifested itself in his deeds.

"Nasty customer," said Alec. "What's his background?"

"He was a Welshman from Monmouthshire, which is only across the River Wye from the Forest of Dean. He always insisted that he was a gentleman's son of good quality, as he put it; but it seems that his father was a farmer. He enrolled in the army when he was in his teens, and was sent to the Caribbean. A war was going on there with the Spanish and he took part in the capture of Jamaica. When the war was over he left the army and became a privateer."

"What exactly was a privateer? Wasn't it the same as a pirate?"

"Not quite. The countries that had colonies in the Caribbean tried to get rid of pirates - of all nationalities. But they accepted privateers provided they didn't ravage their own countries' ships and settlements. Privateers considered themselves a cut above common pirates. They thought of themselves as private armies - or navies. And the British ones attacked only Britain's enemies - mainly the Spanish - so I suppose you could say they did a service for their King and Country, as well as for themselves."

"Sounds like Drake to me," said Alec.

"Yes, I didn't realise that this privateering had gone on from Drake's time through the 17th century up to Morgan's."

"I suppose these privateers were really only taking from the Spanish what the Spanish had plundered from the native peoples out there. But go on."

"Well, the Caribbean was infested with privateers at this time. They used Jamaica as a base. They repaired and equipped their ships there, and that's where they unloaded their loot when they returned from their raids. Jamaica's economic health depended on them. The arms dealers, the victuallers and the ship builders thrived when the privateers came back into port - to say nothing of the grog shop owners and the whores who relieved the men of their prize money."

"Sounds an interesting place," said Alec. I smiled to myself. Alec was the mildest man I knew. He would run a mile to avoid a prostitute. But I continued.

"The Governor of Jamaica used to encourage them. He issued commissions to go out and attack Spanish ships. These commissions were given on the understanding that the loot would be surrendered to the authorities. The crew were allowed to keep items of small value, like clothing and small arms, and I expect more valuable articles were unofficially shared out by them before the ship returned to Jamaica. When they reached Jamaica the goods were sold, usually quite cheaply, and the money from the sale, along with the coin and bullion they had captured, was divided among the people who had a claim to it."

"Who were they, apart from the privateers?"

"First the Governor took one fifth for the King and one tenth for the Duke of York as Lord High Admiral. Then he took a share for himself; and about a quarter went to people who had supplied equipment and goods on credit. The rest was divided among the officers and crew. The officers, of course, got a larger proportion than the men. Some of the officers invested their money in slaves and plantations. Most of the crew spent theirs in the taverns and brothels in Port Royal."

Alec got out his pipe and lit up. I could tell by the way he settled back in his chair that I had him interested. "Tell me more about Morgan," he said.

"As I say, when he left the army he became a privateer. It was perhaps the most lucrative thing he ever did. He spent ten years raiding Spanish merchant ships and pillaging Spanish towns and villages on the Main. Then he returned to Jamaica, fit and satisfied with his achievements, and still only 30. He invested the money he had received from his raids in plantations and he got married."

"And settled down as an honest and respectable citizen, I've no doubt," said Alec.

"Yes," I replied. "But the taste of the high seas, the adventure, the fighting and the glory of being a privateer never left him. A few years later the Governor of Jamaica asked him to lead a force of privateers against the Spaniards. He agreed, and as the admiral of a fleet of 12 ships he sailed off to attack Portobello on the mainland. Portobello was the Caribbean port for the city of Panama. It was from here that the galleons, laden with the riches of South America, set out across the Atlantic on their risky journey to Spain.

"He captured Portobello. You must read the details sometime. It was a bloody business. Morgan threatened to set the town on fire unless the Spanish rulers paid a large ransom. They did. They handed over rubies, bars of silver from the mines of Peru and gold coins, and so saved their city. While negotiations were going on Morgan's men were busy torturing the unfortunate Spanish inhabitants and extracting all their money and valuables. Then they departed in triumph. You mentioned Drake. In taking Portobello Morgan had succeeded where Drake had failed 75 years earlier."

I paused. I had never had Alec so attentive.

"The whole of hot and smelly Port Royal turned out to greet Morgan and his men when they returned," I continued. "The booty was shared out and the town celebrated. But in a few weeks the excitement had died down and the men had spent all their money. They pressed Morgan to lead another expedition and he was soon off again. This time it was to Maracaibo in Venezuela, and it was equally successful."

"But didn't the Spanish do anything about these raids?"

"Yes. After the raid on Maracaibo they decided to attack the privateers in their own base, Jamaica. The English there got to hear of the plan and decided on a pre-emptive strike. Morgan gathered together a fleet of 38 ships." I looked at my notes. "His own ship was the biggest. It had 700 men and 22 guns. Altogether under his command he had over 2,000 fighting men.

"This time the destination was one of the richest towns in all America, Panama. It was on the Pacific side of the isthmus. Morgan and his men landed on the Atlantic side and fought their way across and captured Panama. As they entered the city, the Spaniards set it on fire. The slaughter of the Spanish was terrible. Morgan took 3,000 prisoners - soldiers and civilians. Don Perez de Guzman, the President of Panama, fled the city with as many of its inhabitants as could escape. Those that didn't were tortured, poor devils, to find out where they had hidden their wealth.

"However, the booty the privateers captured, even though they raked over the ashes of the smouldering city, was not as much as they had hoped for. And they were frightened that if they took it back to Jamaica it might be confiscated because of a truce that had just been agreed between the British and Spanish governments. So they decided to share it out among themselves before they left Panama."

Alec interrupted. "It seems that Morgan kept some of the spoils back for himself."

"Yes." Again I referred to my notes. "When the men were told the size of the pool - £30,000 plus the value of about 400 slaves - they realised that they would only receive about £20 each. They had won bigger prize money on smaller adventures such as Portobello and Macaraibo, and their mood turned ugly. Was this small sum all they were to receive after a bloody expedition that had lasted eight months and had included ten exhausting days in the isthmus jungle? You can imagine them saying it. They thought that all the loot had not been placed in the common pool, and Morgan was accused of keeping some of it back. Richard Browne, who was Morgan's personal physician, and usually faithful to him, is on record as saying that Morgan cheated the men of a vast sum. On another occasion he reckoned that the real value of the booty was £70,000."

"And I suppose that when things began to get too hot for Morgan he cleared out."

"Yes, he slipped out of harbour quietly one night and set sail for Jamaica. After he left, the rest of the expedition broke up and the ships made their way back to Jamaica independently."

Alec nodded his head.

"The Spanish government in Madrid was, of course, furious over the whole incident. To mollify them the British government had Morgan arrested and taken to England. I couldn't find out exactly what happened to him there, but he doesn't seem to have been kept under any restraint."

"So he had plenty of time to go to the Forest of Dean and check that his treasure was safe."

"True. Three years later when the Spanish had quietened down, he was knighted - that would be in about 1675, I suppose - and sent back to Jamaica as its lieutenant governor! He held that job for about seven years, and then spent the rest of his life in Jamaica in comfortable retirement. He ran his plantations and entertained his friends. He drank heavily, apparently, and grew fatter every day. He died when he was 53, of dropsy. He was an amazing man. He must have been the greatest of all the privateers on the Spanish Main."

All this time Alec had sat looking into the fire. I knew that he had a wonderful capacity to retain and distil the essence of everything he was told, and that he was now mulling over what I had told him.

After a pause he looked up. His only comment was: "That's a pretty good picture of Morgan. What about John Morris?"

"He was an old crony of Morgan's. They had been on joint enterprises together ever since Morgan became a privateer. He sailed with Morgan at Macaraibo and was probably with him at Portobello. He was certainly at Panama. I've even traced the name of his ship. It was the *Dolphin*, just as Morgan says in his letter."

"And how do you know it was Morris who took the treasure to England?"

"I can't prove it," I admitted. "But I've established that all the ships that were on the Panama expedition sooner or later either returned to Panama or were shipwrecked on the way back. Only one was not accounted for. That one could have been Morris's. And he could have sailed it back to England with the treasure on board."

"Could have," grunted Alec, and ran his hand through his hair. I could see that he was trying to find arguments against me, and it annoyed me a little. But I knew that if he accepted my views it would be difficult for anyone else to demolish them.

"What about Robert Burney who Morgan is supposed to have left his treasure to?" he asked.

"Burney was a Yorkshireman, and I've confirmed that he was with Morgan at Portobello and Panama."

"My, you've been working hard. Have you found any proof that Burney saved Morgan's life at Portobello?"

"No," I said, "but the account in the letter has an authentic ring."

Alec grunted and was silent for a minute. Then he picked up Morgan's letter and examined it again.

"The letter is quite consistent with other historical facts that I have discovered," I said. "Apparently the Spanish archives in Madrid confirm that a galleon did escape from Panama with most of the wealth of the city. The men on the expedition did accuse him of stealing booty from the common pool and Morgan did head back to Jamaica when they challenged him about it."

Alec nodded.

"Even the smallest detail is borne out," I continued. "In one of the books I have read there was a letter written by Morgan's doctor saying that in his last years he had dropsy and was much given to drinking. It all ties up. I don't think there's any doubt that the letter is genuine."

Alec smiled, but I could see that he was not yet convinced.

"Here, you read my notes," I said, and handed him a hard-backed folder labelled 'Pirate Treasure'. It may be stupid vanity, but I am proud of the way I always write my notes neatly on ruled sheets of paper - no backs of envelopes for me - and file them in a folder. I was pleased to show them to him.

"My, you *are* neat," he commented, and began to read.

"Meanwhile, I'll get something to eat." Ten minutes later I returned with a tray of sandwiches and hot coffee.

"Well," said Alec, taking his glasses off and selecting a sandwich, "I think you have something here. But, you know, not everything in the letter is supported by your notes. I can't find anything about John Witt, the man who helped Captain Morris to bury the treasure."

"No, I must have forgotten him."

"The letter says he was the Keeper of the King's Coalworks. I should think that was an important job."

"Yes, it shouldn't be too difficult to find something about him. I'll try."

"If we can find out where he lived we may get a clue to where the treasure was hidden."

When Alec said "if we can find out" he usually meant "if you can find out." I made a note in my book.

"And what about the map?" he said.

"There wasn't any map in the box, I'm sure."

"I don't think we are going to get very far without it."

"I don't think we are going to get anywhere at all without it." We laughed.

"Come, we mustn't get too pessimistic!"

"Let's start again at the beginning," I said. "If the treasure was still safely buried when Morgan wrote the letter and no-one has dug it up since, it must still be there."

"That's obvious," said Alec, rather rudely, I thought.

"But I expect Robert Burney dug it up soon after he received the letter."

"Not necessarily. Burney might not have been able to get to England. Of course anyone could have found the letter and the map after they had left Morgan's hands. We don't know when the map was separated from the letter, and even by itself it could have led to the treasure. We don't know what was on it, but there was probably enough to encourage anyone to dig where X marked the spot."

I did not reply. The room was getting cold. It was after midnight, I suppose, but neither of us was conscious of time. Outside the wind shivered in the oak trees and roared down the chimney. I put some more logs on the fire, since it seemed that we would be there for some time yet.

"Let's go through the letter again," said Alec. This we did, line by line, checking every item in it with my notes. We came to one of the holes that Alec thought had been made by rats gnawing at the original manuscript.

"I guess that this gap means that since both Captain Morris and John Witt were dead, when he wrote the letter Morgan was the only person who knew where the treasure was," I said.

"Unless Morris or Witt had told someone before they died," replied Alec.

"You know," I said, "I wish I knew how the letter got into the box at the Record office in the first place."

"It could have come back from Jamaica with a load of other papers that were left when Morgan died, and nobody bothered to read them. Then perhaps they found their way into the Record Office and this one got put in the box marked 'M', again without anyone reading it."

"That would mean that Morgan hadn't send the letter to Robert Burney."

"Yes, and that would mean that the treasure is still hidden somewhere in Dean."

"Yes, but where?" Alec yawned into the back of his hand. We were both getting tired.

I went to the window and looked out. All was now still and quiet. The porch light, which I had inadvertently left on, showed that it was snowing heavily.

"I bet it never snows like this in Jamaica," I said. "You can't go home tonight Alec. You'll never get through."

He came to the window and looked at his car. It was covered with snow.

"You'd better sleep in the spare room," I said. "It's all made up."

So he phoned his wife and we went to bed.

I slept badly that night. Whether it was the cups of coffee I had drunk or the excitement that our discussion had generated, I don't know. When I fell off, I dreamt of pirates, of seeing a Spaniard's head cut off with a swing of a cutlass. As it flew through the air past me, it cried "Pirate Gold, Pirate Gold!" And then I was in the chest Morgan had stolen, along with the diamonds and emeralds. But they weren't hard, they were soft and moist, like soft fruit, and warm, and the chest was being taken down a stony slope in the dark. I could see Morris and Witt as they carried the chest, their faces grim and dripping with sweat. I knew exactly where the place was and I wanted to tell Alec, but I couldn't get out of the chest. I began to panic and tried to force the lid off from inside, but wasn't able to. I woke up, sweating, and couldn't get off to sleep again.

Alec slept badly as well, and it was two bleary-eyed amateur detectives that met in the kitchen next morning and had a brief breakfast.

He left just as it was getting light. There had been a thaw during the night, and though the roads were not clear he managed to make his way home and then to work.

A few days later when I had something to report, I telephoned him and suggested that we should meet for lunch on the following Saturday at the *Winding Wheel* in a Forest village called Bream.

He agreed. "But why Bream?" he said.

"I'll tell you when we meet," I replied.

I knew the landlord of the *Winding Wheel*. It has been modernised now, but at that time it was still an old miners' pub. I liked it. It was cosy in spite of its roughness. The walls of the public bar where we sat were of undressed stone, as they had been for centuries. Tables consisted of long scrubbed boards resting on cast iron supports. As we sat on the wooden benches with our beer and sandwiches, we could sense the presence of generations of miners drinking and joking with their comrades and forgetting for an hour their labours and hardships.

That day there were only four others in the bar, all Foresters. They were sitting tightly together in a corner discussing something that from the occasional outburst of conversation seemed to be most important. Rudely, we listened to catch what it was all about, but we couldn't get the drift. At first, they glanced in our direction, clearly wondering who these strangers were, but when we started talking ourselves they lost interest in us.

"I like this pub," said Alec, as he positioned his sandwiches and beer. "But why have we come to Bream?"

"Because I'm pretty certain John Witt lived here."

Alec's eyes brightened. "You've traced him, then?"

"Yes. Just as Morgan said, he was the Keeper of the King's Coalworks in the Forest and an important man. I think he lived at a house called the Old Place."

"What makes you think he lived there?"

"The Old Place belonged originally to the Gough family. John Witt was married to a Gough. He died in about 1687, a year before Morgan. It all ties up."

After lunch we went for a walk through the old part of Bream. It is a pretty place, or was in those days. I have not been there recently. Small houses, sprinkled with a few shops, bordered on the main street that ran from where the maypole used to stand up to the top of the hill. The houses were not architecturally outstanding, I suppose, though I am no expert. But like pensioners whose active days are over they sat and contemplated, steeped in the sun of ten score summers and hardened by the ravages of ten score winters. I pointed to a building, bigger than the surrounding houses, a handsome structure with stone mullioned windows, elegant dripstones and a fine two storeyed porch.

"That's where John Witt lived," I said.

Alec nodded.

"In the 19th century it came down in the world and became a pub. Nobody lives there now. It's been empty for some time."

We walked up the road.

"So," said Alec, "if John Witt lived in that house, the treasure must be near here, because Morgan says in his letter that it was buried near his house."

I agreed. "Not only that. The letter also says that it was hidden where treasure of another kind had been produced. What does that mean?"

"Perhaps it means the treasure was buried in a coal pit."

"Perhaps, but how can we trace a coal pit that existed in the 1680s? It would be filled in by now and forgotten."

Alec agreed, but I said that I would see if I could find any maps of coal pits near Bream for this period in the Record Office.

"Good," said Alec briskly. I could see that he was now convinced that the treasure existed.

It was some weeks before we met again. Once more we had lunch at the *Winding Wheel*. I had found in the Record Office a map of Bream dated 1692 and had made a tracing of it. I showed it to Alec. The scale was about 3 inches to the mile, but it was no more than a rough sketch. It did, however, have several coal pits marked. They were all in the same area, just north-west of the village, and beneath them was the inscription "Coales have been gott here".

When we had finished our lunch we cleared the plates and beer glasses from the table and, as accurately as we could, inserted the position of the pits on a modern Ordnance Survey map. Then we hurried out of the inn and up the road to where the pits had been.

"After all this time," I said, "I'm sure there won't be any trace of them."

I was wrong. The sites of four of the pits were now under early 20th century houses, but we found two of them in open country. In a field by a hedge were two smooth depressions about two feet deep and ten feet across.

"Bell pits," I said.

"What's a bell pit?" asked Alec.

I was pleased to air my knowledge. "In those days they wouldn't dig very deep. Sometimes they only went down ten or twenty feet. Then at the bottom when they reached coal they would dig outwards until the hole was like a bell. When they had taken all the coal, or when the sides collapsed or they were flooded out, they would abandon the pit and dig again somewhere else. Then the hole would gradually fill in with earth. But usually, even after centuries, they never levelled off."

Alec's comment was brief. "I don't fancy digging down there on the off chance, even if the farmer allowed us to."

It was still half an hour to closing time, so we returned to the *Winding Wheel* and sought inspiration in another pint.

"If 'treasure of another kind' doesn't mean coal, what else could it mean?" I asked.

Alec slapped his open hand on the table, spilling the beer and making two old miners at the next table look up. "What about iron ore?" he said. "They've been digging iron ore in Dean for centuries haven't they?"

I remembered my dream. "Of course," I said. "The Scowles." Grabbing his arm I pulled him out of the pub, across an adjoining piece of waste land, over a barbed wire fence (on which he tore his trousers) and into a wood.

As we went deeper into the wood, the ground became rougher. Grass gave way to an uneven path with boulders piled up on either side. Soon we were in the heart of the Scowles, walking through deep troughs gouged out of the earth.

Bushes clung desperately to cracks in the brown-stained rock. The path between the irregular walls narrowed, twisted tortuously and then widened out to circumvent isolated pinnacles of rock. On the top of the pinnacles we saw yew trees, clinging together, their seed carried there by wind or bird. Unhappy trees, they were. Their exposed roots craved for more life-giving soil than they could find. Discoloured and gnashed into fantastic convolutions, the roots blindly descended and, on occasion, pierced the rock and split it assunder.

Surely, only the hands of giants could have made these precipitous and irregularly shaped labyrinths that twisted in and out among the rocks. But they *were* man-made, the surface workings of the miners who had extracted the iron ore in Roman and perhaps even earlier times. Now, centuries later, the scars remained. Nature had tried to smooth the outlines with green, but the rocks were barren and she had been denied complete success.

No sun reached these depths. The depressing scene could only be alleviated by glancing upwards, where there was light and life. Birds outlined their flight against the blue sky, the winds dishevelled tufts of grass as they clung to ledges of rock; a willow tree, standing on the very edge, reflected the yellow of the sun on its leafless branches.

As we passed on, all was quiet. We could hear only the sh-sh-sh of our shoes through last autumn's deep leaves and the noise of an occasional stumble as we slipped on the wet uneven ground beneath the leaves.

We realised that these were only top workings. When they had removed the ore from the surface, the ancients had been forced to go under the ground for their ore. Here and there, at the bottom of fissures in the rock, were holes which we decided might lead to subterranean tunnels. I noticed one such hole at the bottom of a small ravine. A steep slope leading to it looked as if it had once been a properly constructed path. There had been a path like this in my dream.

"Let's go down to that hole," I said.

Alec looked surprised, but agreed, and we clambered down. The hole was bigger than it had appeared from above, about five feet high and two feet wide. Most of the entrance was hidden by bushes.

We peered in. And then we looked at each other.

"Let's go in," I said.

"Yes, but not today. It's too late and it's getting dark."

"It's dark inside anyway."

"We need lamps. And we must have the right boots."

I was disappointed, but cheered up when Alec said that he had all the equipment we would need at home. I had forgotten that he was an experienced caver.

We agreed to meet at the Scowles the following Thursday morning if we could both take the day off.

"Wear any old clothes, though a boiler suit would be best," said Alec. "The temperature in there is pretty constant all the year round, about 50 degrees, so don't put on any extra clothing. I'll bring some boots for you - we take the same size I think - and I'll bring some helmets and head-lamps."

Thursday was a beautiful day. Birds told us with their singing that this was the first good day we had had since Christmas. Freed from winter dullness, light clouds scudded across the blue sky.

As we approached the hole we glanced round. There was no-one about. Fortunately, visitors to this part of the Forest were rare. We donned our boots, put on our miners' helmets and fixed the lights to them. The batteries - rather heavy, I thought - we attached to belts round our waists. Alec slung a rope across his shoulders.

"We've not much equipment, so we may not be able to go very far," he said. "I've brought some food in case we're down a long time."

We entered the hole, Alec first. I was a novice at this game and was apprehensive at going down into the dark, but excited as well. Within a few seconds we found ourselves in a small cavern about twenty feet across and ten feet high. Our lights disturbed a colony of bats. They fled to a corner and disappeared emitting a high-pitched "tweek". At the back of the cavern was a hole that proved to be a tunnel leading down a slope. We entered it. In a few yards we had to edge cautiously along a narrow path by the side of a deep ravine. On the bottom a river gurgled. There was no doubt that we were on a man-made path, albeit made years earlier. I imagined iron workers in their tassled caps, steadily making their way up it, the path lit only by candles fixed, as was the custom, to sticks in their mouths. But what did it mean to us if hundreds of iron miners had come up the path? The important question was - had Morris and Witt gone down it with Morgan's treasure?

Down and down we went. We left the ravine through a tunnel, and entered a wider area. It was about nine feet high. On either side were enclaves where the old miners had picked the ore out of the veins. We saw scratchings they had made on the walls. These were the oldest workings. Two thousand years ago there would have been life and movement here. The miners, having prised the ore from the walls with their mattocks, would have passed it to women and boys to carry to the surface on their backs.

We continued downhill - we must have been five hundred feet below the surface now - and then we turned into a tunnel under a large rock stretching over the path. Alec, who was few feet ahead of me, stopped.

"Look," he whispered.

I looked over his shoulder, my light supplementing his. Before us, its extremities disappearing into the gloom, was a large cavern, as big and solemn as a cathedral, a cathedral in natural stone. But it was more intricate, more delicate than any man-made cathedral. From a roof, countless feet beyond the shifting shadows cast by our lights, grand pillars hung motionless and silent as they had hung for thousands of years, enormous stalactites of intricate design and fantastic shape, some green, some red, some brown, some pure white like a bride, all as delicate as carved ivory, all glistening with moisture.

Far below on the floor rose columns of stone, some small like dead, branchless tree trunks, others broad and grotesque, all reaching up towards the stalactites above. Down the walls of the cavern, bouncing from ledges and boulders, poured torrents of frozen stone. And all was silent. There was nothing but this glorious sight, fixed in time.

When had this revelation last been looked upon by man? Five hundred years ago? A thousand years ago? Probably never, for no miners' candles could give as much light as our two battery lamps. The difficult climb down had been justified by this vision alone.

As we gazed, the silence was so intense that I could almost hear it. Then it became unbearable. I wanted music to enhance my experience. Music, only music could be added to this sight, only music could mingle with the majesty and dignity of the cathedral and enhance it. Mozart and Beethoven alone could match with their art this magnificence of nature.

And then I committed a blasphemy. To relieve the tension I shouted out, a piercing scream that echoed around the cathedral's walls, up to its roof and down to its depths. My voice came back to smite me.

My shout broke the spell both for me and for Alec. Alec turned and followed the path as it snaked under a ridge by the wall. I remained a few seconds longer, and then followed him.

We trudged on for ten minutes or so. The path continued to cling to the side of the cavern, but it was becoming narrower and rougher. Suddenly I had no wish to go further, and could not understand why Alec was pushing on. Then he disappeared round a corner, and I heard a shout. Fearing that he had fallen, I hurried on. I found him on his knees, but he had not fallen. His cry had not been one of pain but one of discovery.

He looked up at me, his eyes shining bright in my headlamp.

"Look," he said. "Look there." He pointed to a hollow low down in the wall. In it was something covered with dust and barely recognisable as man-made. Alec's sharp eyes had spotted it. We hurried over. It was an enormous chest, about four feet long and three feet high, and was bound with two strips of iron held in position by iron studs. On the front was a clasp and a lock. Above the clasp what seemed to be a metal plate was fixed. I rubbed it with my sleeve. It was an elaborate medallion, with the inscription "J P de G" on it.

"The initials of Juan Perez de Guzman," I whispered. "The initials of the Spanish governor of Panama."

We looked at each other. For several seconds we could not speak. My heart seemed to be in my throat.

"This must be it," said Alec, with a shake in his voice.

To conceal my emotion, I turned to the chest and gingerly touched the lock. It fell away. It had been forced.

"Someone's got here first," I cried. Even so, I tried to open the chest. It had a deep lid, and heavy, and its hinges had rusted, but after an initial jerk it rose easily. I threw it back.

It was as if the sun shone in my face. Reflected in our lights were rubies, sapphires, emeralds, pearls, silver coins and gold coins, piled high in bright disarray, fantastic in their beauty.

Our ecstasy lasted but seconds. There was a rush like a thunderstorm from above. Stones falling from the roof of the cathedral filled the air.

"We must get out right away," said Alec, and seizing my arm he propelled me back up the path. Boulders and stones came down faster from the roof. We thanked God that none hit us, and kept as close as possible to the wall as we hurried along. The climb back to the entrance to the cathedral seemed ten times as long and stressful as the journey down. The reverberating sound of falling rocks pressed against our ears as if all the world was noise. We reached the tunnel at the entrance to the cathedral, and once in its safety we paused to glance back. Large lumps of rock continued to fall, and then, with the thunder of hell, an enormous lump of stalactite decended. It was at least thirty feet across, and must have weighed a hundred tons. It crashed against the path where we had been standing only a few minutes earlier, ricocheted off, and plunged to the depths below. It hit the ground with a thud that shook the whole cavern, and made a noise that must have been heard miles away.

Then my heart turned over. A large part of the path where the lump had hit now splintered off from the cave wall and slowly somersaulted into the abyss. I saw the treasure chest standing on one edge of the enormous splinter. Then it was thrown clear. It twisted in the air, and the lid fell away. The jewels scattered themselves among the pieces of debris that were still descending from the roof and plunged with them to the bottom of the ravine.

Alec grabbed my arm and urged me on. We reached the open air at last and collapsed on the ground, too exhausted to say a word.

That evening we sat before the fire in my house once again.

"Your shouting must have loosened some stones in the roof," said Alec.

I didn't disagree. My mind was on the treasure. "To think that we actually found it, and then it was snatched from us," I said.

"Well, it's still there at the bottom of the ravine," Alec grinned.

"Yes, I suppose we could still get at it," I said, ignoring his attempt at humour.

"No, I think not. I wouldn't go into that cave again, that's certain, and I don't think you would either."

I groaned. "No, I suppose not."

"More important than losing the treasure," said Alec, "is losing that wonderful cathedral. I have never seen anything so breath-taking in my life."

But I was not to be consoled. "There are other caves like that elsewhere, I expect."

Alec laughed. "Yes, you are probably right."

"But we must keep it a secret," he said. "If news gets out, there will be treasure seekers, the press and busybodies with metal detectors in their thousands trampling all over the Scowles and ruining the whole area."

I was silent.

"Do we agree that we say nothing to anyone?" he persisted.

I looked at him.

"I agree," I said reluctantly. "We say nothing."